RELENTLESS

CODE R.E.D.
BOOK 4

CHEYENNE MCCRAY

cheyennemccray.com

1

His life was based on lies.

Zane Steele rubbed a hand over his jaws, his gut tightening as he studied the blonde sitting on a park bench in the Common.

Sunlight winked through the trees and caressed the woman's lightly tanned arms and legs. A light summer wind lifted her sun-streaked hair from her shoulders.

Boston might be a little on the humid side this morning, but his throat was completely dry as he watched her eat an ice cream cone, her tongue darting out delicately as she licked the ice cream.

Zane hitched his shoulder up against a tree and found himself unable to take his gaze from her. He shouldn't even be thinking of introducing himself.

This wasn't a one-night stand kind of woman. This was a woman a man would want to come home to at the end of a long day and warm his bed every night. And for Zane, pursuing any kind of relationship while living a life of secrecy in order to protect everyone he knew, was downright insane. But that didn't stop him from staring.

As far as he knew, most RED agents who had relationships with civilians didn't have the same qualms about keeping their real occupation secret from the ones they loved.

He wasn't one of those agents. He couldn't have a relationship based on not being able to share everything with the woman he loved.

Zane pushed away thoughts of commitments and studied the woman slowly licking her way around the ice cream cone. She wore a skirt that landed just above her knees before she'd sat down. When she'd made herself comfortable, the skirt hiked up her thighs just enough to tease. His heart almost stopped when she'd crossed her legs and her skirt inched up higher.

The sound of shoes pounding along the path had Zane looking over his shoulder. Out of habit, he moved his hand closer to his Glock.

It was a male jogger. He passed by and the woman smiled. The jogger acknowledged her with a nod and a wink.

The surge of jealousy that slammed into Zane almost knocked him on his ass.

What the hell?

Goddamn, but she made him want her in ways he'd never wanted a woman before. He wanted to claim her. He wanted to make her his in every way. And not just for one night. He wanted to come home to her, wanted to hold her at night, and he wanted to wake up to her in the morning. And he hadn't even touched her yet.

In the past, he'd refused to take any relationship beyond the mutual understanding that it wouldn't go beyond sex and friendship—pretty much in that order. The woman could never question him on any aspect of his life. If she came to his bed, it was just for fun. Pure animalistic, unadulterated, hardcore fun.

Zane's throat worked again as he watched the woman in

pink slowly run her tongue up the cone as she licked it where it had started to drip.

Well, hell. With this one, he wanted more.

But he didn't want to bring anyone into his life that he would have to lie to every single day for God knew how long. Maybe forever.

The only family member who knew the truth was his younger sister, Lexi, who lived the same life and also worked for the clandestine government agency, RED, the Recovery Enforcement Division. It was an offshoot of the NSA and technically didn't exist. Not even their big Irish family knew what they really did.

Only RED's Director; the Deputy Director; a federal judge; a federal prosecutor; the head of the NSA; Senator Jeannette Shelton; and the President knew. Not even the V.P. or his cabinet members were aware RED existed.

RED had four divisions—Narcotics and Weapons Trafficking along with Weapons of Mass Destruction; Terrorist Activity and Organized Crime; Technology Theft; Human Trafficking and Sex Crimes.

At least when he was in the Secret Service it didn't matter who knew and they just had to understand he couldn't talk about work. Same for Lexi when she was Army Special Ops.

Zane shifted against the tree, feeling the rough bark through the overshirt that hid his Glock. He shouldn't be watching the woman like this. He shouldn't be wanting her like this.

But he couldn't fight back the images of pushing her hair from her heart-shaped face and tasting the perfect fullness of her lips.

He dragged his hand over his jaw again. His informant would be here in the next half hour and he needed to concentrate on his current case. Not on some woman he didn't even know.

.   .   .

WILLOW RANDOLPH DID her best not to look directly at the man who was focused on her so intently.

Law enforcement. He had it written all over him. It was the authority that radiated from him even though he was thirty, maybe forty feet away. It was almost tangible. She felt like she could reach out and wrap herself in all his power.

From beneath her lashes, she saw his throat work as she licked her ice cream and sucked some through her lips. His expression was pained, and she did her best not to smile.

Dangerous, that's what he was. The kind of man who'd be hazardous to a woman's heart.

He had "Bad Boy" written all over him.

She'd bet a month's salary from her job at Macy's—well maybe a week's—that he was something other than a police officer, but still in some branch of law enforcement. Definitely not a desk jockey.

His hands looked strong enough to snap a man's neck yet she imagined that those same hands would be gentle on a woman's skin.

Willow could almost feel his fingers glide over her body.

He was a stranger, but she had the incredible desire to run her hands over his muscular chest and his broad shoulders before she slipped her fingers into his black hair. His carved biceps and strong forearms would hold her tight.

She could picture herself reaching up, wrapping her arms around his neck, and bringing him down for a kiss as she pressed her body close to his. He had a quarterback's build from his broad shoulders to his lean hips, so he would feel hard and strong against her softness.

Maybe it had just been too long since she'd had sex, because the way he made her feel just standing there watching her and the way she was fantasizing about him was insane.

She crunched on her cone while he watched then she slowly and deliberately sucked each of her fingers clean.

Ha. Let him go home and wish he had at least come up to her and introduced himself. Let him wonder what it would be like to be with her and wish he'd had more guts.

Coward.

No, there was nothing in the least bit cowardly about this man. He didn't make decisions without weighing his options.

The man pushed away from the tree he'd been leaning against.

Willow couldn't help it. She raised her eyes and met his. Green. His eyes were such a beautiful shade of green.

The pounding of her heart seemed to rise from her chest to her throat. Swallowing at this moment wasn't an option. She couldn't have torn her gaze from his for the life of her.

Heat traveled through her as he made a more blatant assessment of her. His gaze started traveling over her from her ankles to her nearly bare thighs, up her belly, and rested on her breasts.

Two could play this game.

A breeze teased her hair as she parted her lips. She tasted the sweetness of ice cream on her lower lip as she ran her tongue along it.

How would he taste?

She let her gaze freely roam over his powerful form. Such incredible thighs and muscular build. Just to push him closer to the edge, she let her gaze rest on his excellent package before she met his eyes again.

Willow curved her lips into a wicked smile as she braced her hands to either side of her hips on the park bench.

I dare you, she told him with her expression.

He dared.

2

Zane couldn't have stopped himself if he tried. When the woman gave him that challenging little smile that was all it took.

He never backed down from a challenge.

She looked surprised then almost amused as he walked toward her. When he reached her, she looked up at him and smiled again.

"You've been driving me out of my mind," was the first thing that came out of his mouth.

Her smile turned into a grin. "I know."

Zane wanted to smile in return but instead, he sat a couple of feet away from her on the park bench. He rested his forearms on his thighs and leaned forward, studying her.

Damn, but she was even prettier up close. Her scent carried to him on the breeze and reminded him of an ocean breeze and sunny days as his gaze rested on the curve of those perfect lips. He met her eyes that were such a pretty sea blue it would be like getting on a boat and getting lost for days on the brilliant Caribbean Sea.

"Zane Steele." He used his real name and not his undercover

one as he reached his hand out to her. He only used his real name when it came to personal things.

"Willow Randolph." She took his hand and her warm touch had more than his gut tightening.

It seemed they were both reluctant to part as they slid their hands away from each other. Her touch tickled his palm in a way that made him think of those fingers all over his body.

"Randolph ..." Even as he reveled in Willow's touch, a combination of anger and pain burned his skin at the memory of another Randolph. "My sister, Lexi, just lost her best friend, Stacy Randolph." On an undercover op with RED, he added silently. No one outside RED knew she'd died a hero and not a victim because no one knew she had been a special agent with RED.

Willow's smile faded a little. "Stacy was my cousin. She was one of my best friends, too." Willow sighed as sadness crossed her features. "I'm staying with my aunt and uncle for a while so that they're not alone now that Stacy's gone. She was their only child."

They were both silent for a moment, but they never lost eye contact. Those sea-blue eyes would be easy to get lost in.

"Your accent isn't New England," he finally said. "I'd guess Upper New York."

"You're good." She smiled again and her eyes had an edge of amusement to them again. "But then a cop is trained to notice everything."

A small shock jolted him. He tried to keep his expression from showing how startled he was that she'd come close to nailing him. "What makes you think I'm a cop?"

"Not really a police officer." She cocked her head as she studied him. "But definitely law enforcement."

Shit. If he was this easy to read how the hell had he made it through so many undercover ops?

"Secret Service," he said. He had been SS and everyone thought he still was. "You pegged me. Now I want to know how."

"Ah. Secret Service." She crossed her legs at her ankles. "Taking some time off?"

"Something like that." Funny she hadn't answered his question. He glanced at his watch. His informant should be here soon, and he shouldn't be sitting here having this conversation.

"Are you going to ask me to dinner?" Willow had a clearly curious expression. Not like a woman who expected a man to ask her out, but a woman who was observant enough to know when a man was attracted to her.

Zane put his hands on his knees and straightened. "I'm not so sure you'd want to go out with me."

Willow now looked intrigued. "Why not?"

He sighed and glanced down at the grass at their feet before looking at her again. "I'm not into relationships."

She shrugged. "Who says I am?"

"It's written all over you, honey." Zane put one arm on the back of the park bench. "You don't do one-night stands. You expect to see a man at least a few times before you make up your mind whether or not you want to date him anymore."

"You are observant, Zane." The way she said his name brought to mind thoughts of her saying his name over and over again in bed. "But in other words, you're afraid."

"I've never been afraid of anything, Willow." He got up from the bench seat. Better get the hell out of here.

She tilted her head back and met his gaze. "This time you are."

Willow had just challenged him again. Damn. Even though he never backed down, in this case, it would be the smart thing to do. Real smart.

No one had accused him of being smart all of the time.

Zane glanced at his watch. Henry should be walking down

the path any moment. "It's closing in on noon." He looked up at her. "How about I meet you for lunch at the Irish pub on Province at one?"

Ah, hell. What did he go and do that for?

Willow gave him her beautiful dimpled smile which did damned funny things to his gut. "This is my lunch break and I have to get back to work. Let's say dinner at that contemporary American restaurant and lounge at Stanhope and Clarendon. I'll meet you there."

He stared down at her for a long moment, taking in her unpretentious beauty and the kind of confidence that came from a woman who was comfortable with herself and her choices. This woman was dangerous to him in more ways than he could count.

Zane found himself giving a slow nod. "Seven?"

"Perfect." Willow stood and her skirt slid back to just above her knees. What a shame. Those thighs were meant to be seen. "I'll meet you in the waiting area."

Their eyes met and held again. "I'll be there," he said.

"I know you will." She turned away and headed toward the downtown area.

He shook his head. You're in deep shit now, Steele.

IN THEIR CORNER of Macy's cosmetic department, Willow hummed silently as she taught her client how to apply a new look with some of their latest products. The cosmetics company she worked for was one of the best.

"It's all in the brush." Willow took a sterile mascara wand from a package in a pocket of her black smock and handed it to Mrs. James. Willow would toss the wand once the woman used it. "This side lengthens while this end of the brush thickens and separates."

"What an interesting concept..."

Willow's thoughts wandered, Mrs. James's words turning into white noise as she thought about Zane.

Zane Steele.

Being close to him had left her feeling charged and needy all at the same time. He'd smelled so good that she could almost taste him. Earthy, male. And his deep voice had sent delicious shivers down her spine when he'd said her name.

"You're up to something." Linda passed by in a wake of their brand of perfume that smelled of freesia and magnolia blooms. "I can see it in your eyes."

Eyes. Oh, Mrs. James.

"I'll tell you about it later," Willow said to Linda as she took the mascara wand from Mrs. James and threw it into a wastebasket. "It's the finishing touch on really bringing out your eyes," she said to the woman who was probably in her fifties but now was appearing more like she was in her early forties thanks to the cosmetics.

Next, Willow showed Mrs. James how to apply her blush and then her lipstick.

She couldn't help her thoughts turning to Zane and picturing his powerful build and the way he made her feel just by being close to her.

Oh, yeah. That man was Danger with a capital D.

"Willow?" Mrs. James's voice brought Willow out of her daydream. Which had to be at least her tenth daydream since getting to work.

The woman batted her eyelashes as she looked at herself in the huge lighted mirror. "I love it." Mrs. James smiled at her reflection and looked even prettier. "I can't believe it. What a transformation."

"Beautiful," Willow could say with complete honesty. The gradual change in Mrs. James's appearance was like watching a bud bloom into a full-fledged rose. "What interests you the most out of everything?"

Mrs. James didn't even pause. "All of it."

Cool.

"I'll get your product for you and then ring you up." Willow left Mrs. James admiring her own reflection, obvious delight in her gaze.

Willow couldn't resist taking a crumpled piece of paper out of her pocket and taking a shot into the wastebasket by the stockroom door. "She jumps, she shoots, she scores." The paper ball landed dead center in the wastebasket.

"That's a three-pointer if I ever saw one," said the chic, completely fashionable Linda just before she entered the doorway of the stockroom ahead of Willow.

"Nothing but net, baby," Willow said.

"Terrific job on that lady." Linda reached for a box that contained liquid foundation off a shelf while Willow pulled out her products for Mrs. James. "Now tell me what the smiling, humming, and daydreaming are all about."

"I met a man today." Willow smiled and then winked as she added, "A real man."

"Hmmm." Linda's stylish chin-length black hair swung forward as she searched for a particular shade of blush in a long row of boxes containing blush compacts. "Does he have any brothers?"

"I'll find out." Willow grabbed the last shade of eye shadow she needed. "Tonight."

Linda drew out a box containing blush then turned to Willow and raised her perfectly arched eyebrows. "You never go on dates."

"That's because I hadn't found the right man." Willow

backed out of the stockroom, checking over her shoulder to make sure she didn't run into anyone. "I think I need to do a little more investigating."

Linda smirked and still managed to look beautiful. "Uh-huh. You just found a guy you'd like to sleep with."

The grin that flashed across Willow's face was something she couldn't help. "If you saw him, believe me, you wouldn't be calling him a 'guy.'"

"What does this man do?" Linda asked as she stepped away from the shelf.

Willow laughed. "Would you believe he's in the Secret Service?"

"No way."

"Yup." Willow juggled the armload of products for Mrs. James. "Spotted Zane as law enforcement the moment I saw him in the Common."

"Secret Service Agent Zane, huh?" Linda cocked her head. "Sure he's not full of—"

"Absolutely."

"Complete report expected tomorrow afternoon." Linda swept past Willow. "You're not allowed to spare any details, so have a great time. And I'll live vicariously through you."

As if Linda had any shortage of guys.

But not a real man.

"Knock him dead, Willow." Linda's voice carried over her shoulder as she headed to the cash register with her hands full of products.

Willow smiled.

That's exactly what she intended to do with Zane tonight.

Knock him dead.

Or maybe...just knock him into bed.

3

"Zane." Lexi rapped on the doorframe to his office at RED HQ and he looked up from the intel that he'd been staring at but hadn't really been seeing. "Jeez, where are you?" She folded her arms and leaned her back against the doorframe. "I knocked twice. Not like you to zone out like that."

"Work." Yeah, like he was going to tell his younger sister about the woman who just wouldn't get out of his head. "What brings you from the fifth to the second?"

Lexi worked in Human Trafficking and Sex Crimes on the fifth floor of RED's five-story building on Portland Street in Boston. Fourth floor was Terrorist Activity and Organized Crime; third floor Technology Theft; and then the second, Zane's floor, Narcotics and Weapons Trafficking. The first floor was admin, but also served as their front—an insurance claims processing center.

"I needed to see Georgina." Lexi glanced over her shoulder to the Command Center which was a lot like the CCs on every floor. "She hasn't been at home when I've stopped by her apartment the last couple of days, and I can't get a hold of her on her personal cell."

"I sent Rizzo undercover." Zane closed the manila folder he'd supposedly been looking at. "There's an arms deal going down that we got wind of and she's the right agent for this job."

"If she comes in, tell her I need to talk to her." Lexi gave a mischievous grin. "It's really important."

"Probably has to do with your partner." Zane gave a wry look. "You and Donovan spend plenty of time working together."

If his former Army Special Ops sister ever blushed now would be the time. "Nick Donovan and I are Team Supervisors who happen to be paired up."

"Uh-huh." Zane leaned forward, his forearms on his desk. Before Lexi could get in another word, he said in a subdued tone, "I met Stacy Randolph's cousin today."

Sadness and pain flashed over Lexi's features and any trace of teasing was gone. It had only been a few months since Agent Randolph had been raped and murdered on a case where Lexi had sent her undercover. Stacy had been Lexi's closest friend.

"Her cousin Willow." Lexi gave a slow nod. "I talk to Mrs. Randolph every now and then. I haven't met Willow but it's pretty nice of her to stay with Stacy's parents."

Zane couldn't say anything because the next words he'd have said might have been, "She's so damned beautiful and fascinating that I can't get her out of my head." But he managed to keep his mouth shut.

"Don't forget Mama's making bangers and mash on Sunday." She gave him a teasing grin. "When you go out with Willow, ask her if she'd like to come."

His jaw almost dropped. "What—"

"I'm your sister." Lexi started to turn away. "From a mile away, I could see that you've got a thing for her."

Well, hell. If two women could read him so easily in one day, he might as well turn in his credentials.

For at least the hundredth time, Zane wondered why in the hell he was here at the restaurant bar waiting for Willow.

And for at least the hundredth time, he thought of how beautiful and intriguing she'd been.

He took another swallow of his mug of Guinness on tap. His gaze never left the doorway as he leaned against the bar and waited for her to walk through. He'd come a half hour early, needing a beer before he saw her again.

There was something about that woman that drew him. Maybe she wouldn't be the same intelligent, insightful woman who had captured his attention. Maybe she wouldn't be as beautiful—

He just about dropped his beer.

A supermodel stepped through the doorway of the restaurant.

Willow.

Zane barely registered the fact that he'd left a twenty in his empty beer mug as he slowly walked toward Willow. She was beautiful to begin with but now he knew the true meaning of the word 'stunning.'

She had the same unpretentious smile, the same casual confidence as when he'd met her. But now she looked like she could be on the cover of some chick magazine. Hell, the cover of the next Sports Illustrated swimsuit issue.

Willow wore some kind of little black dress that he didn't notice so much as the amount of cleavage and thigh it exposed. The same smooth golden skin, the same sun-streaked hair the same long legs. It was more the sexy wave of her hair and the way her sea-blue eyes looked bigger, her lips even more delicious.

Damn.

He'd known he was in trouble before, but now he didn't have a doubt that he was in deeper than he could swim.

Zane hit some guy's shoulder with his own, but he didn't even bother to mumble an apology to the guy because he was too focused on Willow.

When he reached her, she continued to smile at him as she tipped her head back. At six-two, Zane only had about three inches on her. She was as tall and willowy as her name. Somehow he hadn't noticed that before, and he was trained to notice everything.

He was slipping all over the place when it came to this woman.

"I reserved a table for us," he managed to get out as he stared at her and drank in her scent that made him think of sunny days and an ocean breeze.

"Good." She slid her hand into his, interlocking their fingers. "I'm starving."

Zane tried to ignore the out-of-control sensations pinging through his body at the feel of her fingers locked with his. "I thought supermodels didn't eat."

Willow laughed. An honest, friendly laugh that did more funny things to his gut. "Grad student and part-time cosmetologist," she said as they reached the hostess who was waiting with a pair of menus. "Most definitely not supermodel."

"Could have fooled me," Zane said as they followed the hostess to a corner table.

THE WAY ZANE had looked at her sent a shiver of delight down Willow's spine. She could read so much from his eyes. Definitely desire, but genuine interest in who she was and not just in her appearance.

Talk about appearances. Good lord, he was gorgeous. Just like she'd remembered from his broad shoulders and chest to those carved biceps and strong forearms. Those were arms made to hold her tight.

The hostess took them toward a corner table in the red-brick walled restaurant that was elegant yet contemporary.

She squeezed Zane's hand tighter, and he rewarded her with the sexiest smile that made her sigh. Even the smells of lobster, steak, and other delicious meals didn't appeal to her as much as Zane did.

He wore a dark green shirt with an overshirt, probably to cover his weapon. But he had another weapon he couldn't disguise behind his jeans.

Zane's short black hair had the slightest wave to it that made her want to run her fingers through it. Yeah, she'd do that.

The hostess showed them to the perfect table for two in front of a tall rectangular window. The atmosphere in their part of the restaurant was romantic and only added fuel to the incredible fire burning within her.

He looked like he hated to release her hand as much as she didn't want to let his go, but he did and pulled out her high-backed cushioned chair for her.

"And you're a gentleman, too," she said as he seated himself.

The hostess left the menus and said something about wine but neither of them paid attention to her.

Zane focused his gaze on her. "Honey, if you knew what I was thinking right now, you wouldn't think I'm anything close to being a gentleman."

Willow picked up her menu and gave him her best naughty grin. "Then you and I must be thinking the same thing."

At first, Zane looked taken aback but then he had a teasing

glint in his eyes. "That I have great breasts and the most gorgeous legs you've ever seen?"

She laughed. "I know what you're really thinking." She leaned close to him. "Instead of being in this restaurant, you'd rather be in bed. With me."

He cleared his throat. "If I could make it that far."

"Ha." Willow looked at her menu before looking over the top of it at him. "Let's see if we can make it through dinner."

Zane picked up his own menu. Cleared his throat again. "Not sure I'll live that long."

"You know what?" Willow settled her hand on his knee and slowly moved her fingers up his thigh and kept her tone low. "They have two very private, very elegant, very clean restrooms here. With locks on the doors."

Zane raised his eyes from his menu, a hungry, primal, and pained expression on his face as she inched her fingers upward to what she really wanted to touch.

"When the server comes, you order our appetizer and wine and I'll get up and go to the ladies' room." She skimmed her fingers over his thigh. "You follow me as soon as you finish ordering."

Zane glanced around them before looking back at her. "Uh, Willow—"

She gave him another wicked smile. "I dare you."

4

Not a second after Willow flashed that naughtier than hell grin the server came to the table. For a moment Zane forgot the server as he watched Willow get up and slowly walk toward the ladies' room.

That tiny little dress barely covered her breasts and ass. His mouth watered.

"Sir?" The waiter's voice was barely enough to bring Zane out of his fantasies. Damn. He'd been doing that all day and it probably wasn't going to stop until he had her. "Wine? Appetizer?" the server asked.

"Uh, yeah." A sudden rush came over Zane as images of being with Willow kept repeating over and over again in his mind. He tried not to look in the direction Willow had disappeared as he picked the first thing his gaze landed on. "Oysters. Wine, you choose."

"Yes, sir." The server gave a slight bow. "I'll bring your wine to you shortly."

"No rush." Zane rose and strode toward the restrooms as soon as the server turned his back.

Half of him knew this was crazy, that he was out of his ever-lovin' mind. But his other half said "get lost" to the first half.

Zane's heart rate had jacked, and his body burned with fire. Willow better not have been teasing him because he'd die if he couldn't have her soon.

It seemed forever before he reached the women's restroom, and he jerked the door open. The moment he stepped through, Willow was on him. She wrapped her arms around his neck and brought him to her for a rough, hard kiss.

He barely remembered to shut the door behind him and press the lock before he grabbed her by her ass and she wrapped her long legs around his hips.

She wasn't wearing any underwear.

A growl rose up in Zane's throat as he swung around so that her back was against the door. She moaned into his mouth before she drew away and pulled down the front of her dress, freeing her breasts.

Hungry for all of her, Zane licked and sucked her nipples. It was so easy to tell she was trying to hold in her moans and cries as she squirmed and rocked her hips against his.

"I've got to be inside you." He raised his head and kissed her before he said against her lips, "Ican't wait any longer."

"Yes," she clamped her legs around his hips and gripped his shoulders. "I've been wanting you all day."

Someone tried the door handle and it jiggled, but Zane didn't give a crap about anything than finally being where he belonged.

As Willow held on, he unfastened his jeans. It was only a slight relief to finally have his erection free. He jerked a condom out of his pocket and had that sucker on in two seconds flat.

He kissed Willow hard to swallow her cries as he thrust hard and buried himself in heaven.

IT HAD BEEN AN INSANE IDEA, but Willow thrived on impulse and instinct.

Zane drove his erection into her and thank God he kissed her so hard because she couldn't help the scream of pleasure and pain at the unexpected thickness and length of him. She could almost swear he touched her belly button with every thrust.

He didn't ease up as he moved his mouth from hers. She tried to hold back her gasps and cries as he moved his mouth to her ear. "I wanted to take it slow and easy with you our first time, honey. But now I can't have you hard or fast enough."

"Don't even ask me to think because my mind took a hike." She kissed him and her breathing was rough, her words hard to get out. "The only thing that matters is how good you feel." She bit back another cry. "Zane. Oh, God, I'm about to lose it."

The door handle jiggled again and that sound, knowing that people were on the other side of that door as Zane took her, threw her over the top.

This time she dove for his mouth and let him take her cries as the most powerful, most incredible orgasm of her life tore through her. Her body shook and trembled and it felt so good as Zane didn't stop and drew out her orgasm. Her core contracted around him and every throb caused her body to jerk and her mind to hum.

She'd bet Zane held back a shout of his own when he came, and he came hard. He threw back his head, his jaws clamped shut, his face dark as he fought for control.

He was so big that she felt every pulse and throb of his orgasm.

Willow collapsed against Zane, her arms around his neck.

She felt weightless and lightheaded, and she wondered how she was going to be able to walk out of here.

There was a jiggle then a knock at the door. "Hello?"

"Just a minute," Willow said. "I'm having a little problem from something I ate."

"Oh." The woman's voice sounded like she was having second thoughts about using the restroom. "Okay. Hope you're all right."

Willow sniggered as she pressed her face against Zane's shirt. "Actually, I haven't had a chance to swallow what else I'm hungry for."

Zane groaned and she felt him thicken and lengthen. "We'd better get out of here before I take you again." She drew back and looked at him with a sly smile. He clamped his hand over her mouth, a dangerous glint to his eyes. "Don't you dare."

She could barely hold back a laugh as he slid out of her and set her on her feet. She also almost fell because her knees were so weak and her heels too high. When Zane steadied her, he tossed the condom and arranged himself as she tugged her dress back into place and tried to make her hair look like she hadn't just been taken up against a wall. Door. Whatever.

When they'd washed up and were ready, as ready as they could be, Zane said, "There might be a whole line of women out there."

Willow reached up and kissed him. "Don't worry. I've got that covered."

Zane snorted while he stood in the bathroom as Willow locked the door behind her and she started saying things that would drive away any crowd. "Smells just awful...plugged up...need to get management."

He shook his head, then waited a few heartbeats before opening the door and thanking God that no one was in the hallway. Willow had done a good job of scaring away the mob.

His body stilled hummed and burned with heat as he headed back to the table. The fact he'd just taken Willow up against the door in a restaurant's restroom just about blew his mind. He hadn't done anything as daring as that since his young, wild days. Even then what he and Willow had just done made everything in his past seem tame.

Zane approached the table and watched Willow as she spoke with the server. She approved the wine before the server poured two glasses and then he left the bottle on the table as Zane sat.

Damn, Willow was beautiful. He couldn't help smiling at how her hair was a little ruffled in the back. The just-got-laid look only added to her stunning beauty.

"You chose well." She smiled while he pulled up his seat, candlelight from the holder in the center of the table flickering over her features. She circled the rim of her wine glass. "A 2018 Chardonnay."

Yeah. The waiter probably picked the most expensive wine in the store, but he didn't give a shit. All that mattered was the beautiful woman he couldn't take his eyes off.

He raised his glass as she did, but she got to the toast before he did. "Here's to fabulous restroom sex in one of the finest restaurants in all of Boston."

God, this woman made him want to laugh and smile and grin—things he rarely did, especially in his line of work.

They sipped and he raised his glass. "My turn." She brought her glass close to his as he said, "Here's to meeting in the Common one of the most beautiful, genuine women in the world."

Willow flashed her dimpled smile, and he knew he was

getting deeper and deeper with every moment they spent together. The thing was, he couldn't imagine not seeing Willow again, not being around her whenever he could.

He set his wine glass on the table and rubbed his temples. What happened to no relationships, Steele?

"You're scared again, Zane." Willow spoke in her easy, direct tone. He looked at her and she had her arms folded on the table in front of her as she leaned forward, her expression clear and thoughtful. "You're worrying you'll end up caring for someone."

5

———

The server appeared with their oyster appetizer and settled it on the plate, saving Zane from having to respond to Willow. The woman was too observant for her own good.

Zane couldn't take his eyes off her as she handed the server her menu. She was so damned beautiful. But what mattered to him more was her unpretentiousness and even her directness when she asked questions he didn't want to answer.

Vaguely he heard Willow tell the server, "I'll have the salmon with the creamed spinach and the sautéed mushrooms as sides."

Zane sucked in his breath and took a glance at his menu and just chose whatever struck him first. "Surf and turf, the filet medium rare." He returned his menu to the server. "Mashed potatoes and asparagus."

When the server left, Zane continued to study the beautiful woman across the table from him. He couldn't keep staring at her. Even though his body still felt flushed with his orgasm and he had hardened again, he had to say something.

"You know what I do for a living." *Liar.* "What about you?"

"I have my Mister Ed and I'm working for my Doctor Ed."

She smiled and he raised his brows. "That just means I have my master's and I'm working on my Doctorate in Education."

She continued and added, "I'm fifth year ABD at NYU. All-But-Dissertation. I'm working on my dissertation while I'm in Boston, and then I'll go back to NYU to present it before a committee."

"Dr. Randolph." Zane offered her the plate of oysters on the half-shell. She took a couple and put them onto her plate. "Has a nice ring to it."

He took a few oysters himself as she replied, "So does Special Agent Steele."

"You said you were on your way to work when I met you at the park." *And I was about to hook up with an informant regarding an arms deal.*

Willow shrugged. "For the time being, most afternoons I work at Macy's in the cosmetics department. Once I have my doctorate, I'll start looking for a position somewhere on the Eastern Seaboard."

Zane didn't have a clue about cosmetics and wasn't sure he wanted to. "Any place in particular that you'd like to end up in?"

"I really love Boston. I always have." That dimple again. "Before Dad left, we'd travel to Boston from Buffalo so that he could visit his brother, my uncle."

For the first time since Zane met her, a troubled expression crossed Willow's features. "Dad...a couple of years ago he ran off with a 'cute little thing' who's younger than me."

The troubled expression disappeared like a shadow replaced by sunshine when she changed the topic. "I have two bickering sisters, considerably younger, and they still live in Buffalo with Mom."

"They're in college?"

She shook her head. "Twins in their senior year in high school. Wendy and Sarah are ten years younger than me." She rested her forearms and gave him that compelling, insightful look. "I'll bet you're the oldest brother, whatever your family size."

"How do you do it?" Zane met her sea-blue gaze. "Read people."

"I see it in your eyes." Willow tilted her head to the side. "You worry about them and anyone else you love and care for."

Zane cleared his throat. He didn't like the direction this conversation had headed. "I have a very large Irish Catholic family."

"Ha! I knew it," Willow said with a grin. "How many brothers and sisters?"

"Four brothers, two sisters." Zane couldn't help smiling in response. Her grin was so infectious. "Mama and Papa have been married for almost forty years."

Two servers arrived with two large trays of their dinner and loaded the table with all the dishes they'd chosen. Willow took a couple of sips of wine until the servers finished and left.

"Hmmm." Willow spooned creamed asparagus onto her plate next to her salmon. "Bet everyone in your family lives around here and you get together regularly."

"Every Sunday the whole mob shows up at Mama and Papa's. Except Ryan who's in the Marines." Zane cut a piece of his filet. Before he knew the words were coming out of his mouth, he said, "Would you like to come to lunch with my family this Sunday?"

You are one screwed up SOB, Steele. What happened to no relationships? You're moving way too fast, buddy.

Willow's brilliant smile did such strange things to his gut that made him crave one smile after another from her. "Great. I have Sunday off."

Zane started cutting his filet. "Mama is going to love you and

I'm sure Lexi would like to see you. She was...close to your cousin."

"Cool." Willow took another sip of wine. "Can't wait to meet all of them. Bet your mother fixes great Irish dishes, too."

"She bakes one hell of a Shepherd's pie." He shook his head at the same time. "But honey, as far as betting goes, I'm not betting with you on anything again."

WILLOW SLIPPED her hand into Zane's and smiled up at him as they walked outside into the summer evening.

The way Zane looked at her—entranced, yet the fear of relationships was constantly in his eyes.

A mystery, yes, but she'd bet it had something to do with his job. He didn't have the look of a man who'd been burned—because he'd never let himself get that far in a relationship. He ran before it got too serious.

She might just have to change that.

"Where are you parked?" His smooth deep voice flowed over her, and it gave her delightful shivers.

"I took a cab."

"From West Roxbury?"

"I hate driving in Boston." She ran her hand from just below her breasts to her hip in a slow movement and watched his eyes follow her hand. "And I wasn't crazy about riding the T dressed like this."

Zane had that hungry look in his gaze again. "You'd better not ever ride the T dressed like that."

Willow leaned her head against his shoulder as they walked, and he squeezed her hand tighter. "Oh, yeah?"

"Yeah." His voice sounded concerned and possessive all at

once and she wondered if he realized it. "I'll take you back to your aunt and uncle's."

"I have a better idea." She tilted her head to look up at him. "Why don't you show me your place and we'll finish what we started."

She wondered if he realized he was squeezing her hand so hard or that she was holding her breath for his answer. "It's a mess."

Willow drew him to a stop at the corner near the parking garage. She looked at him, meeting his gaze, wishing she could see his green eyes better. "I'm not interested in what your place looks like. I'm interested in you."

In the dim light coming from a nearby lamppost, she saw his throat work. Then he caught her completely off guard by releasing her hand and holding her face in his palms. And he kissed her.

Not a wild, hard kiss like his powerful kisses in the restroom, but gentle and demanding all at once. The moans rising in her throat came out like a soft purr as she moved her hands to his hard chest and explored his muscular pecs, shoulders, and biceps as his tongue moved with hers and they tasted one another.

His flavor was masculine and delicious, and included a hint of the wine they'd been drinking. And lord, his scent. So male with a touch of a musk-scented aftershave.

Zane lightly bit her lower lip then kissed her harder, even more demanding as he moved his hands to her waist and drew her close and tight against him. Willow sighed into his mouth and brought her arms around his neck. She slipped her fingers into his black hair and ruffled it just like she'd been wanting to all night.

The heavy rise and fall of his chest brushed her breasts. He kissed her long and hard until she started to feel dizzy.

"Yeah." Zane broke their kiss and stared down at her before he took a step back and captured her hand in his again. He sounded out of breath when he spoke. "My place. Before I take you right here on the street."

"The street, huh?" She ran her free hand over his chest and felt the rapid beating of his heart. "That's not such a bad idea," she said, knowing mischief was in her eyes, her expression.

Zane immediately clamped his hand over her mouth and his tone was almost dangerous. "You'd better not dare me again, honey, because I might just take you up on it."

6

With Willow sitting on the other side of the console, fire coursed through Zane's body as he drove his Chevy Silverado to his home in Quincy. Images of taking Willow in every way possible kept rolling through his mind and he had to grind his teeth to keep his focus on the road.

He glanced at Willow. "You don't strike me as the type of woman who meets a man in the Common and goes to bed with him the same night."

Her dimple was easy to see in the glow of the dashboard lights as she smiled. "Like my friend Linda says, I don't even date much less have sex with strange men."

Zane had to force himself to keep his eyes on the road before he glanced at her again. "Why me?"

"The moment I noticed you watching me, I felt a connection." Willow raised her slender arms and drew her hair over her shoulders before she lowered her hands to her lap. She looked at him with frank honesty in her eyes. "A connection that I've never felt with anyone."

He tried to swallow but his throat was too dry as he looked back to the road. "I told you I don't do relationships."

"Why?" she asked with clear curiosity in her voice. "What is it you're afraid of?"

Zane couldn't believe he was having this conversation with any woman. Yet with Willow, he felt comfortable for the first time in telling the truth.

He looked at her and then the road again. "My job is dangerous and the people I care for could be in just as much danger if they knew the truth."

"You're not actually Secret Service." She said it with such ease and lack of judgment. "You're with whatever agency Stacy was in."

Zane almost stomped on the brake from the shock that tore through him. He cut his gaze to her. "What did Stacy tell you?"

"Nothing, really." Willow shrugged. "I just knew she wasn't an interpreter no matter that she could speak nine languages. I had no doubt she was in some branch of law enforcement."

He focused on the road long enough to make sure he was in the right lane and not about to roll his truck thanks to the shock.

Willow clasped her hands around her knee. "It was in the way she always sat facing a doorway when we would go out to lunch, the way she observed everything and everyone around us without actually looking like she was doing it."

Damn.

"Stacy had a kind of tenseness about her on some days but other days she would be relaxed, and it was obvious she was truly enjoying herself," Willow said. "That was mostly at her home. She didn't like to go out of the house much when she wasn't at work."

Zane didn't say anything. He didn't know what to say that wouldn't just compound the lies he already lived.

Willow stared out the window at the dark scenery streaking by. "I asked her about it once and she almost choked on a bite of chocolate cake. She denied it of course, but I could see the truth in her eyes, along with a touch of fear—for me because I'd guessed."

When he glanced back from the road Willow was studying him again. For the first time, he saw true pain in her gaze. "Tell me Stacy didn't die randomly. That she wasn't just in the wrong place at the wrong time. I won't ask anything else, and I won't say a word to anyone. I just need to know."

What could he say? Zane only knew he couldn't lie about Stacy to Willow.

He waited a couple of heartbeats as he gripped the steering wheel. Finally, he met Willow's eyes and managed to get out the words. "Special Agent Stacy Randolph died a hero."

"Thank you." Willow whispered the words as she looked at her hands in her lap.

Zane cleared his throat. "My—one of the agents found the sonofabitch who did it and made sure he got what he deserved and then some."

"Lexi." Willow nodded and his heart almost crumbled for her when she wiped a tear away that had streaked down her face, and she kept her gaze on her lap. "Stacy talked about Lexi a lot, and I knew she'd take care of whoever killed my cousin."

"If everyone was so damned observant as you," Zane said as he glanced at Willow, "we'd be in deep shit."

Her smile was still a little sad as she raised her eyes to meet his. "I wish her parents knew she wasn't just another victim and that she probably has a blank star on the wall."

Zane's muscles tensed so much his entire body felt coiled. "It's dangerous for you to know as much as you do."

"I have no intention of letting anyone else know that I made a few guesses about the truth." She wiped at both of her eyes and gave a soft laugh. "I don't even know enough to have it tortured out of me."

"Don't even talk about things like that." Zane ground his teeth and reached for her hand as he drove with his other.

Willow interlocked her fingers with his and squeezed. "I understand, Zane. Just know that with me you don't have anything to be afraid of."

"I have everything to be afraid of," he said quietly.

THEY REMAINED silent the remainder of the way to Zane's house, their hands joined and resting on the padded console as he drove.

Their conversation played through Willow's mind as she thought about Stacy and the dangerous life she must have led. And that Zane lived now.

When he came to a stop in front of a colonial style home, he parked, climbed out, then went around to her side and helped her out of his big truck. When her feet were firmly on the sidewalk, Willow found herself staring up at Zane, his hands resting on her waist.

His eyes were shadowed in the darkness that was relieved only slightly from a nearby streetlight. He just looked at her for a long moment before she reached up and kissed him. At first, he seemed hesitant, almost like he was afraid she would break. But then she drew him into the kiss and his hunger and strength of his need flowed through her.

He needed her.

She needed him.

Not in the sexual sense, but in the soul-deep sense.

Although the sex was a must.

Zane drew away, his expression as dark as the night and just as easy to read.

The doors locked almost silently as he used the remote before he took her hand.

Willow said, "It looks like a nice street."

"I'm not home a lot, but the neighbors watch out for one another." Zane continued to hold her hand as they went up the front stairs. "It's a nice community."

When they finally made it into the house, Zane didn't give her much time to take in his living area and kitchen. She only caught a glimpse of hardwood floors, leather furniture and granite countertops because he immediately flipped on a light that illuminated the stairs and began leading her up.

Three open doors led off the upstairs hallway and Zane took her to the farthest one. She caught a glimpse of a darkened weight room and a small, tiled bathroom on the way. He flipped another switch and soft light illuminated the room from either side of what was definitely a master bedroom. It was entirely masculine. Thick, rough natural pine furnishings and a stone fireplace with a pine mantle, along with wood blinds and wood flooring gave it a rustic look. The colors suited him, too. Forest green bedding and throw rugs by the fireplace and bed.

"This is not what I'd call messy," she said as she looked up at him.

He shrugged. "You should see Lexi's house if you want to see a mess." Zane gave a quirky smile. "I have a cleaning service come in once a week. Lexi needs one daily."

The covers on the bed were pulled back, and her heart started beating faster as he led her to it. He maneuvered her so that she was sitting on the edge of the bed and he knelt and eased off each of her heels.

She thought he was going to take off her dress, but instead, he guided her so that she was on the bed lying on her side and watching him watch her.

"God, you're beautiful, Willow." Zane looked almost help-less. "And not just on the outside."

"Whether or not you believe it, Zane Steele," she said softly, "so are you."

She didn't take her eyes off him as he kicked off his boots before slipping out of his overshirt. He removed his shoulder holster and put his handgun into the drawer of the nightstand next to the bed.

Then he slid onto the mattress so that they were both on their sides, fully clothed, and looking at one another. Not touching, just being.

Her gaze traveled over the power in his body, his defined biceps, corded forearms, and strong hands. His thick black hair was a delicious contrast to his green eyes that held fire and warmth, danger and excitement—and fear.

It was the fear that tore at her heart.

After a few moments, his muscles shifted in his shoulders and arm as he brought his fingers to her face and traced her jawline. His expression was serious, pained. "I'm scared to death, Willow."

She brought her hand to his and felt his warmth beneath her palm. His callused hand was rough over her cheek as she turned her head just enough to kiss his palm before meeting his gaze again. "Don't be," she said.

Zane brought her hand to his chest, over his heart and she felt the strong rapid beat through his shirt. "Feel that?" His throat worked as he swallowed. "It would break if I fell for you, and anything happened that would take you away from me."

7

Willow's own heart jerked at Zane's words, and she felt his fear for those he cared about and his loneliness straight to her bones.

An unexpected sensation twisted deep in her belly, and she realized it was her feeling the same fear for him—that something might happen to him like what had happened to her cousin. She pushed back those thoughts and concentrated on the man she was with. The man she wanted to soothe and make love to.

Willow moved her hand to his powerful shoulder and felt the ripple of muscle beneath her palm as he let her slowly push him onto his back. She eased herself up and onto him so that she was straddling his trim hips, her short dress hiked up her thighs. She wasn't wearing panties and his jeans felt rough between her thighs and she could feel the bulge of his erection pressed against her.

They looked at each other for a long moment before she brought her lips to his. The kiss was slow and more erotic and sensual than any of their rough and demanding kisses. This one held no demands, only the gentleness of two people learning about each other.

Zane ran his fingers up and down her bare arms, making her nerve endings feel alive, on fire, and she wanted to feel those incredible hands all over her body. She grew almost dizzy from his touch, his kiss. His rugged scent filled her, his taste drugged her, the warmth of his body wrapped around her.

Willow drew away and smiled before she reached behind for her zipper and eased it down. The dress was silky on her skin as she pulled it over her head, the material soft yet causing her nerve endings to tingle even more. The dress slid from the white sheets like a dark waterfall that shimmered to land on the floor.

He looked up at her with an expression that might be something like wonder.

"How many times can I say how beautiful you are?" He reached up and cupped her breasts in his palms. "Everything about you."

"Shhh." Willow eased down his body so that he had to release her, and she was low enough to unfasten his jeans. She brought his zipper down. Good, he didn't have on any boxers or briefs. She hadn't noticed in the restaurant's bathroom. All she'd been able to concentrate on then was the feel of him inside her.

She released him from his jeans and he almost seemed to sigh with relief that the tough cotton wasn't strangling him anymore.

Willow shimmied just a little bit further down and Zane groaned. Then he sucked in his breath when she licked his erection like she'd been licking the ice cream cone when they first met.

"Damn." Zane reached for Willow and ran his fingers through the strands of her hair before catching his breath as she sucked.

He looked at Willow as she knelt between his thighs and groaned as her lips slowly went along his length and back up again. Watching her go down on him was so erotic he had a hard time breathing much less holding back one hell of an orgasm.

"I don't want you to stop, honey," he said in a voice that sounded rough and raspy. "But I want to be naked and feel your soft skin."

Willow smiled around him and he groaned again as she rose and let his erection slide from her mouth. She licked her lips. "You're asking an awful lot by making me stop," she said with a teasing glint in her eyes.

Zane let out a low rumble as he reached down, grabbed her by her upper arms, and dragged her to him at the same time he sat up. Yeah, had to lose the jeans. In a hurry.

He kissed her first before maneuvering her so that she was sitting on the edge of the bed. Then he stripped out of his socks, jeans, and T-shirt. Before he had a chance to do a damned thing, Willow knelt on the throw rug by the bed, her fingers wrapped around his erection.

"Now where were we ..." She smiled as her eyes met his. "Oh, yeah," she said before she took him into her mouth. His knees threatened to give out as she licked and sucked.

He'd never experienced anything like this before. It wasn't just sex.

What the hell was it then?

Zane slipped his hands into her silky hair. "I'm about to come in your mouth unless you stop." He watched her face, and she stayed in the moment and only increased the friction of her mouth and hand.

"Open your eyes." His voice sounded so damn rough. "Look at me."

Willow did, her gaze meeting his.

That was all it took to slam him over the edge.

Zane shouted the intense sensations of pleasure that were so good they were almost painful. Willow continued sucking until he couldn't take any more.

WARMTH FLOWED through Willow as she looked up and into Zane's green eyes and by the expression on his features, she saw how much pleasure she had given him.

"Come here." He reached for her upper arms, drew her up, and wrapped her in his embrace so that they were skin to skin, her head resting on his shoulder. "Thank you," he said in the same raspy voice. "Now I'm going to return the favor."

Willow looked into his eyes and saw a dangerous glint in them. Excitement swirled in her belly like a windstorm. With a growl, he grasped her in his arms and moved so fast her head whirled. The next thing she knew she was on her back on the cool white sheet, her head resting on a pillow, and Zane's head between her thighs.

A gasp escaped her as he ran his tongue along her center, catching her by surprise. He slid his hands under her and raised her legs so that they were over his shoulders. She felt the powerful play of the muscles in his back and shoulders beneath her thighs and calves. The roughness of his callused hands beneath her sensitized her skin even more.

But it was his tongue and mouth that had most of her attention. The way he licked her could easily drive her out of her mind.

Willow barely realized she was gripping the sheets so tight with her fingers that her knuckles ached. Her cries grew louder the harder he worked her with his tongue. She almost screamed when he plunged two fingers into her core. They were such a tight fit—like he was—and it felt so incredibly good.

She squirmed from pleasure that tingled everywhere possible on her body, and she knew that when she came there was no telling what would happen. She might explode for all she knew.

Willow gripped the sheet tighter in her fists and her thighs trembled as her orgasm rushed forward. "I'm so close, Zane. So close." Her words were almost cries as she said them. She could swear he was teasing her until she shouted, "*Please.*"

Zane thrust his fingers in fast and hard then sucked her.

She lost it.

The scream that had wanted to escape her when he'd taken her in the restaurant tore loose this time. Her body vibrated and trembled and she felt sparks in her mind and body. Thought wasn't even possible. Only feeling.

Willow gradually came down to earth, back to the room, and looked at Zane, the corner of his mouth curved into a smile.

"Damn, you do scream loud, honey." He glanced over his shoulder like looking around the neighborhood before he brought his gaze back to hers. "Just wait until they hear you when I fuck you."

8

"I love the way you say that." A thrill tingled within Willow that went beyond her orgasm as she watched Zane slip her legs off his shoulders.

"Makes you hot?" His hard sculpted lips curved in a dangerous way as he rose. He moved up her body and braced his hands to either side of her. "When I say I want to fuck you?"

"Yes." She looped her arms around his neck and looked into his green eyes. His thick black hair was ruffled, and his muscles shifted beneath his golden skin from his shoulders down to the hard slab of his torso. "Just hearing your voice does funny things to me."

He cocked one of his black eyebrows. "I'm not so sure I like the idea of being funny when it comes to sex."

Willow grinned. "You know what I mean."

Zane's answer was to lower his head and capture her mouth with his firm lips. He took possession and kissed her with hunger and need. Since the moment she met him, his masculine scent never failed to seep into her pores and capture her. Breathing wasn't easy when he drew away. Everything about him stole her breath.

"You are addictive." Willow lowered her eyelashes, moved one hand to his shoulder, and trailed her fingers over the power of his biceps that flexed beneath her touch. She met his gaze again. "I think it would be hard to get enough of you."

She'd wondered if he might back off, if her words scared him, as if she was demanding some kind of commitment.

"You say exactly what you think, don't you, honey?" He teased her lips with his, letting his stubble brush against her chin. When she didn't answer, he added, "I like that in a woman. Opinionated and decisive—just be sure you remember to be careful."

His expression remained dark and predatory and he kissed her again.

Willow savored his warm masculine taste then pulled back enough to say, "I'm careful. Usually."

Zane gave her a *yeah-sure* look, and she smacked her palm against his arm. "I am careful."

"You lead with your heart, not your head. Believe me, it's not a bad thing. It's sexy as hell. But hanging around somebody like me—*that* could get you killed." He drew back, the look on his features so much darker and more dangerous that it gave her a little shiver.

To erase the train of worry going through his head, she trailed her fingers down his taut abs. She didn't go any further as his expression changed to one of want and need.

"Yep." She sighed. "It's definitely going to be impossible to get enough of you."

So, there.

She'd said it again. Now what would he do?

His expression remained half-hunger, half-worry, but his eyes burned into her as if he might be trying to see exactly what lay in her heart. "I know exactly what you mean, honey."

"You feel good over me like this." She explored the corded

strength of his shoulders and arms that were taut from holding himself above her. At the same time, she kept her gaze fixed on his, wanting to read his thoughts and his feelings in his eyes as easily as he seemed to read hers. "And earlier…I don't think I've ever felt anything like the way you felt inside of me."

His gaze darkened even more as if he was reliving what they'd done in the restaurant. "It was better than I'd dreamed of how good it would feel to be with you. And it was goddamned sexy taking you in that restroom."

She traced one of her fingers from the center of his pecs and moved her hand slowly down, all the way to the hard ridges of his abs. Zane's body tightened beneath her fingertips as she let them travel to his erection again and this time she skimmed her fingers along its length. She watched his jaw clench and the burning fire in his eyes that seemed to flame hotter as she started stroking him.

"Goddamn it, Willow." He closed his eyes for a moment as she lightly ran her nails along him. "I want to go slow with you, but you make me want to just drive into you and take you hard and fast like at the restaurant."

He groaned as he watched her run her tongue along her bottom lip. She brushed her moistened lips over his. "What's stopping you?"

"You deserve better." His voice came out in a deep rasp. "I'd like to make love to you for hours. Taste every part of your body, your smooth skin. But right now, all I can think about is taking you."

"We can save the slow for later." She hooked her arms around his neck so she could draw him closer. "We have all night."

"Neither one of us is going to get much sleep if I have my way, honey."

She smiled against his lips. "I don't mind you having your way with me."

Zane's growl was low and primal as he pressed himself against her. She couldn't have held back the soft moan that rose in her throat if she tried.

"I love how tall you are." He lowered his head and licked one of her nipples, causing her to gasp. "You're the perfect height. And your legs are so damned long. Let me feel them around me."

His hips were firm between her thighs as she crossed her ankles behind him, over the smooth skin of his taut backside.

"That's it." His voice sounded harsh, pained, as he rocked back and forth, rubbing his erection along her center. "The first time I saw you, I imagined this."

"I could see it in your eyes." She raised her hips so that he was pressed tighter against her. "And it made me want you in every way possible."

"You were a goddamned tease with that ice cream cone."

She grinned. "Yup."

"Like they say, paybacks are a bitch." Zane ran his tongue over one of her nipples and then the other.

Willow moaned and arched her back, wanting him to lick and suck them. She wanted to shout how much she wanted him. *Right. Now.* But she knew he needed to feel he had at least this much control.

"I can't take this anymore." Zane reached down and put his erection at the entrance to her core before he braced himself again.

She caught her breath as he waited two heartbeats and then slammed inside her and she cried out. "Oh, God. I'd forgotten how long and thick you are."

"Is that a good thing?" he said as he moved in and out in slow, torturous strokes.

"Uh-huh." With every stroke, she felt how big he was and she raised and lowered her hips in time with his thrusts. "No vibrator on earth could compare."

DESPITE THE FACT sweat was rolling down the sides of Zane's face and he was nearly in pain from holding back from driving in hard and fast, he almost laughed. "Better than a vibrator, huh?"

Willow wiggled beneath him. "Even the ones with the little ears."

Zane snorted from trying to hold back a laugh and then one escaped him anyway. He pressed his forehead against her collarbone. "You are something else, honey."

"Yeah, well, I'm someone who wants you really bad." She squirmed beneath him. "I think I'll pass out if you don't get to— get to—"

"Fucking you?" He raised his head and looked down at her with a grin before he stated, "Can't say it, can you?"

"Just do it!" Willow looked like the sweat rolling down the sides of her face were actually tears of pleasure and pain.

Zane decided to have mercy on her—and himself—and began driving in hard and fast.

"Yeah. Oh, God." Willow tilted her head back and her chest rose and fell in harsh breaths. "That's what I want. Don't you dare stop or I'll show you that I'm capable of violence."

Zane almost snorted again and choked back a laugh. Who knew great sex could be so much fun, too? But he didn't stop if he wanted. He kept up a steady pace, ramming into her as deep as he could go and enjoying the feel of heaven.

. . .

WILLOW HAD THOUGHT nothing could be more exciting, more intense, more fabulous than that restaurant sex. But this—this was blowing everything she'd ever imagined out of the water.

As Zane took her, she felt like heat rushed up and down her skin in waves. He was so big, so long and thick, that the walls of her core felt every thrust, every movement he made.

He wasn't moving fast or hard enough as far as she was concerned. She raised her hips up to meet his every thrust and wriggled to feel even more friction.

She met his gaze and her body started to vibrate. His green eyes focused so intently on her like she was the only thing that mattered to him in the world at that moment.

Just that look, the depth of passion in his eyes made her orgasm rush toward her in even a hotter wave that burned her as she climaxed.

Willow let loose a cry that had to be heard for miles. One that would have the neighbors calling the police because they thought someone was being murdered.

As she came close to passing out and everything grew darker, she now knew what the French meant by "la petite mort," an orgasm being a "little death."

She fought to remain conscious as she experienced the most amazing thing she'd ever felt. Waves and waves of heat washed over her body as she shook. She gasped as she became fully conscious, her entire being trembling, as Zane continued his relentless thrusting.

Then he shouted, "*Oh, shit,*" before pulling out of her.

At first, confusion sparked in Willow's orgasm-fuzzy mind as he came on her belly.

"Tell me you're on the pill," he said at the same time he collapsed and rolled them both so they were on their sides, facing each other.

She smiled as she saw the concern in his eyes while he used the sheet to wipe her belly. "I am."

"I've been tested, and I've always used a condom—until right now." He looked up from what he was doing. "So, you don't have to worry about that. Should have thought to tell you before you went down on me."

"I just donated blood a couple of months ago." Willow couldn't help a grin. "But I haven't been with anyone for a very long time. It's pretty much impossible to contract anything when you haven't had sex for a couple of years."

"What the hell?" Zane stopped wiping her belly. "You've gone two years with no sex?"

"At least." She shrugged. "I just never met the right person that remotely interested me."

"And then you have sex with a man you don't even know on the same day you meet him." He let the sheet drop back onto the bed and he moved his hand up to caress her hip. "That's awfully dangerous, honey. Like I said before, you lead with your heart."

"Okay, okay, you're right." She trailed her fingers over his jaw, his stubble rough beneath her sensitized fingertips. "But I also knew my instincts were dead on when it came to you. I didn't have a single doubt in my mind that you're a good man, and that this would be right."

"Thank you." Zane cupped the back of her head and drew her to him for a hard kiss. "But you're not allowed to pick up strange men ever again."

Willow raised her brows. "Oh? And who's going to stop me?"

"I'll figure out a way," Zane said before he rolled her onto her back and took her again.

9

"Aunt Becky, really, it was okay." Zane had just dropped her off five hours ago, at three in the morning, but Willow was wide awake and exhilarated. She crumpled a paper napkin and made an easy shot into the kitchen waste can. Two points, easy. "Zane's Lexi Steele's brother and—"

"But you didn't know him." Becky set a plate on the breakfast bar with scrambled eggs, sausage links, and toast which smelled so good Willow's mouth watered. She climbed onto a barstool and swiveled on it as she lost a little steam under her aunt's gaze.

Becky put her hand on one of her portly hips. "Staying out until three a.m. with any man the first day you meet him isn't safe."

If she truly had an idea of exactly what Willow and Zane had been doing until two-thirty in the morning—Willow wasn't sure she wanted to know how her aunt would react. No, make that Willow *definitely* didn't want to know.

"Well, now I've met and had dinner with Zane. And we spent a lot of time talking and getting to know one another." Well, some of the time. Willow folded her arms on the breakfast bar. "And I know he's a good guy."

Becky sighed and adjusted the clip at the back of her silver-shot blonde hair. "Secret Service, right? That's what Stacy said." A sad look settled on Becky's features like they always did when she mentioned her daughter.

Willow swallowed back the desire to tell Becky that Stacy had died for her country. Everyone thought it was a case of being in the wrong place at the wrong time, a random act of violence. It was so unfair that no one outside of whatever agency Stacy worked for could know the truth.

Becky straightened and Willow met her aunt's hazel eyes. "You've been an angel to stay with us these past few months and helping out like you have with your job at Macy's." Becky reached up and put her hand over Willow's. "But you have a life to get back to."

"I'm enjoying being here with you, two," Willow said and meant it.

Becky squeezed her hand. "For the Lord's sake, child, you've done everything but defend your dissertation to get your doctorate. You keep putting it off to stay with us. You need to go back to NYU, do your thing, and start applying for a position doing what you're so good at. Helping people."

Becky drew her hand away and her smile showed she was proud, sad, and frustrated with Willow. "Just imagine the lives you'll be touching. The positive impact you can make on so many futures."

"I want to be here for you right now." Willow glanced around the large, eclectic living area that she could see from the breakfast bar.

A place that would never have the grandchildren running around that Stacy and her fiancé would have had. Stacy and Barry had planned to start a family—she was going to be quitting her job as "an interpreter" to start her new life with her future husband.

Now that future was gone. No grandchildren would be terrorizing this house or their grandparents' cranky poodle.

Willow met her aunt's eyes. "Would you rather I leave?"

"Lord knows I love having you here." Becky's eyes grew a little watery and she busied herself wiping down the kitchen counters. "But you're putting your life on hold when you need to be living it."

"Right now, I'm where I need to be." Willow picked up her fork, but her hand shook for some strange reason. "I need to start preparing again to defend my dissertation anyway, and I can get busy on that in the mornings while I work in the cosmetics department in the afternoons."

"Then promise me this." Becky carefully folded the cloth she'd been wiping the counters with and set it beside the stainless-steel sink. "After your daily morning run, you will go to the library every weekday morning with your laptop and do whatever polishing up you need to on that big paper, the dissertation. And schedule a date to go to New York City and be done with it." Becky's gaze was firm, determined. "No more keeping me company in the mornings before you go to work. I'm fine."

Willow gave her aunt a faint smile. "Can you and I still have Saturdays together as our day?"

"Until it's time for you to move on." Becky looked so much younger when she smiled. "Absolutely."

"Good." Willow looked at her plate and back to her aunt. "How about breakfast? Can we still chat over your wonderful dishes?"

"Of course." Becky reached up and stroked Willow's hair over her shoulder before letting her hand drop away. "I want you to promise me one more thing."

Willow tilted her head to the side. "What's that?"

Becky gave Willow "the eye" that said she wasn't fooling around. So many times, that look had scared the crap out of Willow and Stacy when they were kids. Willow had to fight the urge to squirm on the barstool.

"No more picking up strange men in the Common," Becky said in a firm tone.

Willow smiled as she thought of Zane, who'd actually never left her thoughts at all. "I've heard that somewhere before."

ZANE DRAGGED his hand over his jaw. He hadn't managed to get much sleep after he'd dropped off Willow and he'd forgotten to shave this morning. One glance at the glass wall of his office and seeing his reflection told him he looked like shit.

He couldn't get images of her off his mind. Willow looking fresh and pretty while she sat on a park bench in the Common eating ice cream; then Supermodel-stunning at the restaurant; and best of all how she looked after she'd just been taken. Her features flushed, her lips parted and swollen from his kisses, her hair messy on his pillow, and looking at him with pleasure and trust.

Trust. Zack looked out through the glass wall and toward the Command Center with its rush of activity with agents working on cases. The hundreds of monitors and screens gave the whole floor a blue glow. Goddamnit, Willow was too trusting, and it was going to get her into trouble.

What are you going to do about it, Steele?

Zane rubbed his temples with his fingers. That was a question he wasn't ready to answer even though that answer hovered at the edge of his mind.

Why'd he agree to have lunch with Willow today?

Because she deserves more than a one-night stand.

And because he had to see her again. Her smile, the honesty in her clear blue eyes, the fact she said whatever was on her mind, and her unpretentious beauty—*damn*.

Last night, before he'd dropped her off at her aunt and uncle's home, they'd agreed to take it a little slower.

Now he was regretting that agreement like hell.

"Knock knock."

Zane looked up to see Georgina Rizzo at his door. The agent showed every bit of her Italian ancestry in her striking looks. Those looks had gotten her a long way undercover. She was not only beautiful but a damned fine agent.

"Are you all right, Steele?" Rizzo wore what looked like an incredibly expensive red silk blouse along with a tailored black skirt that came to mid-thigh. Her long dark hair hung in waves around her shoulders, and she wore large hoop earrings that were obvious pure gold. She was the poster girl for the perfect Italian mafia girlfriend.

She tossed her hair back in a way that was sure to grab a man's attention. "Just wanted to stop by and give you a report before I headed back out into the jungle."

"Everything okay?" Zane pointed to a chair in front of his desk.

Rizzo gracefully sat in the chair, crossed her legs at her knees, and casually draped her arms on the armrests. "At least Albano Petrelli is a gorgeous bastard of a Mafioso Capo Bastone."

"So, you're in good with the underboss?" Zane reclined in his own chair. He didn't have to worry about Rizzo being followed— she was too good of an agent for that.

"Of course." Georgina held out her hand and examined her red nails before putting her hand down and giving Zane an amused look. "Albano didn't know what hit him once I got a hold of him."

"What's up with the arms deal?" Zane said.

"The arms the Petrellis are selling?" Rizzo said. "They're Barrett 82A1 .50 cal. armor-piercing."

High-capacity semi-auto rifles. *Shit.* Zane rubbed his temples again. "Okay, we've got specs on the shipment. But I still don't have time, location, and who they're selling weapons to."

"Oh, but I do," Rizzo said with a wicked smile. "One a.m. Tuesday morning at the Klein warehouse." She got to her feet. "Albano's totally in lust with me so he doesn't worry if I'm around when he's talking business." She frowned. "And get this. They're selling the weapons to a terrorist faction led by a man named Hisham Nasri."

"Fuck." Zane ground his teeth. "Since when did the Italian mafia start trading arms with terrorists?"

Rizzo scowled "When the terrorists offered more cash than the Petrellis make pushing dope, they went for it."

"I doubt any of the other families are going to be happy about this if they find out."

"We might just have to leak that info," Rizzo said.

Zane nodded then studied Rizzo for a moment as he thought of what she had to do to get this intel. "Damn, I hate putting female agents in this kind of position."

"But with male agents would be okay?" Rizzo rolled her eyes. "Friggin' double standards with you men. Just like Nick with Lexi."

Then Rizzo winked at Zane. "Like I said, though, Albano's hot. I can handle him." She shuddered. "It would be worse if I had to snort coke or if he shot me up with that drug, Lascivious, and tried to share me."

"If we're looking for a positive that would be it." Zane rubbed his hand over his jaws again. "Excellent work, Rizzo. Just watch your back and your front."

Georgina Rizzo gave Zane a sultry look as she put her hand

on her hip. "Baby, you're the only one for me," she said in a way that would send most men to their knees. Then she laughed. "Gets Albano every time."

Zane held back a groan. Georgina Rizzo was a close friend of his sister, Lexi, and that made it even harder to send her out in the field. Especially after Lexi's best friend, Stacy, was murdered. He had to get his head back in professional mode and not personal.

"He thinks I'm out shopping." She held up the red purse that matched her blouse and looked even more incredibly expensive than her clothing.

"Just wait until Wickstrom gets a load of my expense report for this purse and other clothes I had to buy before I got into Albano's graces." Rizzo opened the clasp of her purse. "Check this out." She tilted her purse so Zane could get a good look and he shook his head at the enormous roll of hundred-dollar bills. "Baby, I love to shop. No hardship here."

Dick Wickstrom was the ASAC, Assistant Special Agent in Charge, for the narcotics and weapons department, and a tigh-tass if there ever was one.

Rizzo managed to make Zane smile at the same time he shook his head. "Get to shopping then. And be careful."

"I'll be in touch next time I have something to report." She turned and looked over her shoulder. "Otherwise, I'll be out shopping."

By damned, they got what they needed. Now he just had to prepare teams of RED agents to come down on the warehouse to make the bust.

After having watched Georgina Rizzo walk out the door of his office it hit him like a hammer to the gut. Rizzo's undercover assignment made him remember just how dangerous his occupation was. He withdrew his personal cell phone. He should call Willow and cancel their lunch date.

Then he remembered that of all things, Willow didn't carry a phone. She'd said it was because she didn't believe in them. He'd have to change that, too, so she'd have one for emergencies.

Zane pinched the bridge of his nose. The more he thought about her, the more possessive he felt.

Not a good path to head down, Steele.

If only he could get whatever it was in his chest to agree with him every time he thought of Willow.

10

Friday, three days after they'd met, Zane sat across from Willow at a deli on School Street. She was a lot like his sister—unapologetic when it came to eating in front of men. No prissy girl picking at her food to look like she didn't eat much. Willow ate with enthusiasm and enjoyment.

She was so pretty with her sun-streaked hair, her smooth, heart-shaped face. Every movement she made was graceful. Taking her to bed was what he thought of every time he saw her. Hell, even when he didn't see her, he fantasized about her long golden legs wrapped around his hips, her slender arms linked around his neck when she brought him down for a kiss.

No, pretty didn't describe her. Beautiful wasn't enough either. So much about her made it difficult to explain just how special she was.

And he loved to watch her no matter what she was doing.

"What?" She looked up from her thick barbeque pork sandwich. A touch of barbeque sauce was at the corner of her mouth.

"A little sauce." Zane reached across the table and wiped the sauce away with his thumb, just to skim his fingers over her face. She always smiled when he touched her and every time her smile did something to his chest. An ache, a longing that told him he was in deep shit.

She moved her lips just enough to draw Zane's finger into her mouth and suck. He nearly groaned out loud.

Willow let his now wet finger slip from her mouth. "Don't want to waste any," she said with a wicked glint in her eyes.

God, he wanted to take her now. But they'd agreed to slow things down and they'd only had lunch together every day since that incredible dinner and night afterward. Because Willow spent Saturday with her aunt, she would spend Sunday with him and his family, then him alone.

It was the alone part he was looking forward to.

"Sunday, when you meet Lexi, please don't mention that you have any clue that Stacy was more than an interpreter." Zane held her gaze. "You and me, that's it, okay?"

"Okay." Willow spoke in a subdued tone now. "I just wish I had someone I could talk with who could tell me more about what Stacy really did. I just want to know because she was so special to me."

"I'm sorry." Zane leaned close, over the table and kept his voice as soft as hers. "But you need to understand how dangerous any knowledge can be."

Willow sighed and set down her sandwich. "It's hard."

"I know, honey." He gripped one of her hands that was on the table. "You don't know how hard it is for me, too. Especially when something like that happens."

She gave a slow nod. "I don't have to like it, but it is what it is."

Zane leaned back in his chair. "How's the preparation to defend your dissertation going?"

"You remind me of my aunt." That was something Zane wasn't so sure he liked hearing. "Every day she presses to make sure I'm preparing and not off doing something 'impulsive' like she says I do a lot."

"Like meeting me?"

Her lips quirked. "Yeah, she wasn't too crazy about me going out with a man the same day I met him and not getting in until three a.m. Even though you are Lexi's brother."

"I wouldn't have approved, either." He narrowed his brows. "And you promise to never do it again, right?"

She gave a mock salute. "Yes, sir!"

"About that dissertation."

"I've been going to the public library every day and making my last revisions on my laptop." Willow pointed at her purse that was resting by her feet. It was large enough to hold her laptop, which was both slim and small.

With his memory for details, Zane wasn't surprised he remembered the design was something his youngest sister, Rori, was into, a brand called Coach. Not something Lexi would go for —she wouldn't be caught dead with something designer if it wasn't part of her undercover work.

Willow took another healthy bite of her barbeque pork sandwich. "Can't wait to meet everyone in your family on Sunday," she said after she finished chewing. "I just have my younger twin sisters, so it'll be fun to be around a really big family."

"Well, now you'll get almost the whole experience." Zane held his own sandwich, ready to take another bite. "Almost the whole bunch. Our brother, Ryan is Special Ops in the Marines and who knows where he is right now."

"Eight, nine, still big either way." Willow sipped a drink of her lemonade through a straw in her Styrofoam cup. She glanced at her watch before setting her lemonade on the tray on the table. "Hey, gotta run. I'll be late for work if I don't get going."

Zane stood at the same time she did and caught her by the shoulders before he kissed her long and hard as she kissed him back. He wanted to do more than kiss her, damnit.

When they parted, she picked up her purse and gave him one of her smiles that always punched him in the gut and made him wonder what the hell he'd gotten himself into.

"Now I'm really in the Land of the friggin' Giants." Five-foot-four Lexi Steele planted her hands on her hips as she looked from the five-eleven Willow to her three over six-foot-tall brothers. The diamond piercing at her bellybutton winked in the sunlight and Willow wondered what the Chinese symbol meant that surrounded Lexi's bellybutton.

By the spark in Lexi's green eyes, Willow could tell Zane's sister was comfortable with her shorter height and wasn't serious as she glared at everyone around her.

Now Willow could report back to Linda that Zane did have older brothers almost as sexy as he was.

"But I'll take you each on one-one-one," Lexi was saying, and it was obvious she meant it. From what Zane told Willow, Lexi was a small package but she "kicked ass."

"How about we go three on three?" Zane's brother Troy said.

Willow tried to keep a straight face as she rubbed her damp palms on her jean shorts. The afternoon sun and humidity had her pulling her hot pink tank top away from her chest, too.

"Okay." Lexi looked around at her three older brothers, and their twelve-year-old brother who was taller than Lexi. "I'll take Zane and Willow over you buffoons."

Willow high-fived Lexi as she said, "These boys will go down fast."

She wasn't kidding. She'd played ball from junior high

through four years of college and was even asked to try out for several WNBA teams as guard. But for Willow basketball was just meant to be fun, challenging, and her break from studying. It hadn't been her life's ambition.

Within fifteen minutes, after several jump shots, easy passes, layups, and three-pointers, all three of the huge Steele brothers, including Zane, stared at Willow as if she'd come from another planet.

"You've got a ringer." Troy shook his head as he looked from Willow to Lexi. "We should get a handicap."

"I want to be on her side," the twelve-year-old shorter brother Sean said to Zane. "Trade ya."

Zane studied Willow and said, "Not on your life," as if he wouldn't trade her outside of basketball, either.

Heat flushed Willow's cheeks as she stood on the three-point line and palmed the ball. She glanced at Lexi who was grinning.

"Oh, you boys are so going to die," Lexi said with an evil laugh.

Lexi might be five-four, but she weaved around the men with ease and made several of her own jump shots as they started another game of three-on-three. Zane was just as good as Lexi.

The two men and younger boy on the opposite team held their own pretty well, but they never stood a chance.

After destroying the brothers five games to zero, everyone was pouring sweat except for Willow who wasn't really winded just damp from perspiration, mostly from the heat and humidity. She'd never lost her endurance after so many years of playing one of the most demanding sports, that required extensive cardio training and playing.

The five miles she ran every morning was barely challenging. It was mostly to help keep her fit.

Zane put his arm around her shoulders and Willow noticed that everyone around them just about dropped their jaws. Zane didn't seem to notice as he said low enough for her to hear, "You're full of one surprise after another."

"Lemonade and whiskey pie," Mrs. Steele called from the front door.

Everyone picked up their jaws and bolted for the house. "Dibs on the biggest piece!" Sean yelled as he beat his older brothers up the steps and onto the porch.

Willow wanted to lean into Zane, but she could be pushing it in front of his family. Before, they might have thought he'd brought her home because she was Stacy's cousin—now they knew better.

And apparently, this was something Zane had never done before—which didn't surprise her in the least.

She looked up at Zane. "Whiskey pie?"

He gave her one of his heart-melting smiles. "An Irish dessert, of course. Mama grew up on Irish cooking and that's what she serves from appetizers to desserts." They reached the steps. "And not one of us complains."

Including Zane's parents, the nine members of the Steele bunch sat at the incredibly long oak table. The only one missing was the brother who was in the Marines. Willow climbed onto the matching polished oak bench between Zane and Lexi.

Mrs. Steele must have spent at least a couple of days cooking due to the amount of food that had been piled on this table both times they sat down today. Now there had to be enough desserts for each person at the table to have their own pan or platter-full.

"Cool," Lexi said as she reached for a platter with what looked like battered and deep-fried lumpy somethings. "Apple fritters, too," Lexi said.

Ah.

The way the whole family dug in, Willow figured she'd have to jump in if she wanted a taste of the apple fritters and whiskey pie. But Zane slid a slice of pie onto her plate and winked when she looked up at him.

Melt.

God, he was so devastatingly handsome when he did that. He made her feel like warm chocolate and she wanted to pour herself all over him.

Tonight.

Definitely tonight.

11

___

"I love your family." Willow interlocked her fingers with Zane's as they entered his home.

"You loved kicking their asses at basketball, that's why." Zane brought her flush against him as they stood in his front room. "You wouldn't say a word as to how you learned to play so well. What, were you with the WNBA?"

"Almost." Willow smiled as she slipped her hand from his and wrapped her arms around his neck. She leaned even tighter against the hard ridges of his body. He was so warm, and he felt so good and smelled so fabulous. "A few teams tried to recruit me at the end of my four years at NYU. But I opted for concentrating on graduate school instead."

He kissed the corner of her mouth. "What other secrets do you have?"

"You'll just have to find out." Willow reached up and kissed him.

Thrill after thrill started rolling through her belly as Zane grew more demanding in his kiss and the way his hands roamed her body.

"I need you so goddamned bad right now." Zane kissed her

ear, her jaw, her chin, as he unfastened the button to her jean shorts. He pushed her shorts and panties down to her thighs. Zane took her by her shoulders and turned her so that was facing the stone fireplace in his living room. "On your hands and knees on the throw rug."

The excitement running through Willow had her senses on fire as she obeyed. She felt the brush of Zane's jeans as he knelt behind her, heard the zipper—

Then felt the sudden thrust of Zane inside of her.

Willow gave a shout of surprise as he entered and started taking her hard and fast. "You've been teasing me all week." He leaned over her while sliding his hands beneath her tank top and pushing her bra up over her breasts. "Now it's time to get even," he said as he pinched her nipples as hard as he was driving in and out of her.

"I like the way you get even," Willow said, hardly able to get the words out. She might not get winded at basketball, but Zane somehow managed to steal her breath every time they were together.

"This isn't anything, honey," Zane said as he moved one of his hands down and rubbed her between her thighs.

Willow gasped and almost climaxed. It was one of the most erotic things they'd done. Being on her knees with her thighs spread only as far as her jean shorts would allow her to felt delicious. And while Zane took her from behind while still clothed, his rough jeans rubbed her soft skin and stimulated her even more—she could barely hold on.

"I've wanted to be inside you every damned day this week." Zane's voice was a rough growl. "And now I'm going to take you until you're too weak to stand."

"I'm already too weak." Willow moaned as he continued his hard thrusts. "You're going to wear me out."

"Ha." He pinched one of her nipples hard and she moaned

even louder. "You weren't even breathing hard after five games of three-on-three. I think you can handle several good fuckings."

Willow began to tremble as her orgasm came closer and closer.

"Feels so good to be inside you."

"Yes. Good." Willow was almost dizzy from breathing so hard and all the sensations rolling through her body. She couldn't begin to get out a coherent sentence if she tried.

"That's it, honey," Zane said as she trembled harder and nearly crossed her eyes from the power of her oncoming orgasm. He rubbed her sensitive flesh harder. "Come for me now."

This time her cries were like choking sobs as her climax broke through her. She felt as if her body fractured, pieces flying and scattering into shards of glass that glittered all over the floor.

Her arms gave out while he was still taking her and her face pressed against the soft throw rug, her arms above her head. It was a wonder she didn't turn into a pool of hot melted glass.

Willow's body kept throbbing and she jerked with every spasm of her core.

Zane pulled out. "Turn over."

She struggled to move with her trembling arms. As soon as she was on her back, he jerked her shorts all the way off, leaving her socks and running shoes on.

Not even giving her a chance to catch her breath, much less absorb what he was doing, Zane lifted her legs so that her knees were over his shoulders. He had her backside raised off the floor before he thrust deep.

Willow made sharp, gasping sounds. After that incredible orgasm, she was so sensitive inside that she could hardly take any more.

"Oh, you can take more," Zane said and she wondered if she

had spoken the words aloud. "Especially after all of your teasing since I had you in my bed the first time."

"You mean several times."

He groaned as his own body started to tremble against hers. "And you're going to come again."

"What gave you the first clue?" she said between harsh breaths and his grin seemed almost devilish as he looked down at her and pressed his thumb against her center.

Willow shouted this time when she climaxed, and she twisted and turned almost without realizing it.

"That's it, honey," Zane said and a few strokes later he gave a hoarse groan, and she felt him throbbing inside her as he climaxed.

He eased her legs from his shoulders and settled on top of her without putting his whole weight on her. His body burned hot through his clothing to her bared skin, the smell of sex and his masculine scent heavy in the air.

Even as she lay there limp and exhausted, Zane said, "Let's try the table next."

She smiled as she found her second wind.

If Georgina's intel was good, they were just about to make one hell of a bust.

An hour ago, Zane's teams had taken their positions around the dimly lit warehouse. They intended to make sure they arrived before the Petrelli mob turned over the weapons to the faction of terrorists led by Hisham Nasri.

No way in hell was Zane going to let the Petrellis sell the Barrett 82A1 .50 cal armor-piercing rifles to terrorists. Where the hell had the Petrellis gotten their hands on the weapons to begin with?

If anyone could find out, Rizzo could. She'd have to dig deeper.

Zane checked his watch, pressing a button that allowed the screen to be so slightly illuminated that it wouldn't glow bright enough for anyone but him to see.

Inside and outside, the warehouse was wired with RED's high-tech cameras so that every word would be easily heard. RED's techs were the best.

As far as legality for whatever they did, RED had a blanket warrant on this op from the judge who handled all of RED's cases.

Ten minutes to one. The Petrelli family and Nasri faction should be arriving any time now.

It wasn't long before a couple of big dark-colored Cadillacs pulled up followed by what looked like a refrigeration truck.

A few more minutes and three black Mercedes arrived.

Why not terrorize in style?

In moments several men climbed out of each car and walked toward each other. It was almost comical. The men postured and looked like gunslingers from the Wild West.

Two men, one from each group, met halfway beneath one of the pale warehouse lights. Zane moved his binoculars to his eyes and got a good look at the men. From their intel and the photos they'd pulled up on each man, one was Enzo Petrelli and the other man was Hisham Nasri.

Adrenaline began to fire through Zane's system harsh and hot as they got closer to busting the sonsofbitches. And they'd get the head of this terrorist faction—Zane hadn't been sure he'd come himself.

Enzo's voice came through Zane's comm as clear as if the member of the huge mafia family had been standing right next to him.

Zane wasn't sure if he was relieved it wasn't Albano Petrelli because Rizzo would lose her "in" with the Petrelli family if it had been. On the other hand, he could have pulled her out if it was Albano and they busted him.

Enzo was saying, "We've got the goods if you've got the cash." He gestured toward the white truck. "Check the merchandise and we'll take a look at the money."

The terrorist had a hard, angular face and a cold, calculating expression. His accent was strong when he spoke. He mentioned the amount they were paying was in the case they'd brought.

Nasri then inclined his head to one of his men to check the truck. The back door rattled, the sound loud in the night as it rolled up to show crate upon crate.

Zane and his teams just needed to make sure what was in those crates.

Enzo had one of his men go through the briefcase of cash while he and Nasri had a stare-off.

The teeth-grinding sounds of nails screeching against wood cracked the stillness, then the hard thump of a wooden lid. One of the men shouted to Nasri and held up one of the illegal rifles.

Nasri and Enzo shook hands.

"Go!" Zane said into his comm and RED agents began swarming the area with shouts of "Police!" the universal word for law enforcement.

It became obvious in a hurry that Enzo's and Nasri's men didn't intend to go down without a fight.

Zane joined his teams and fury roared through him as he picked off one of Enzo's men who shot a RED agent.

Enzo, Nasri, and a few of the other men raised their hands while the others now lay dead around them.

It was only moments before the men were cuffed and all weapons and cash confiscated.

Two RED agents were down.

Zane shouted orders to team members, telling them what to

do while he and three other RED agents ran toward those who'd been shot. Two RED ambulances had been waiting not too far from the warehouse and drove up at the same time Zane reached one of the agents.

He dropped to his knees and carefully removed the agent's helmet.

By the wide, unblinking eyes, the pale skin, and the stillness of her body, Zane didn't have to be told that Peters was dead. The bullet that pierced her throat had probably severed her spinal cord, and by the amount of blood covering her neck, she'd probably died from both injuries.

"Fuck!" Zane shouted. The RED paramedics were at his side in a second and Zane probably didn't need to say it, but he did anyway. "Peters is gone."

Goddamnit but he could blow a hole through the head of every one of those assholes who were cuffed and now being shoved into vehicles as they were taken into custody.

"Jacobs took a round, but he'll live," Yanov called to Zane. "He got hit full in the chest, but they weren't using armor-piercing bullets."

Thank God for that. Still, Zane's hand shook as he closed Peters's eyes and let the paramedics take her away.

He stood and watched for a moment as his teams efficiently cleared the site of any remaining evidence. That included taking down cameras and listening devices.

RED operated solo and through incredibly strong channels and people in high places, The organization kept off the radar of any other law enforcement agencies. RED had ways of warning off local LE from their ops, and RED agents "took care of business" in smooth, quick, and exact precision.

It wasn't long before all the bodies and blood were taken care of, and the site was left looking like it had before the transaction and the raid.

Tires crunched over gravel as an agent drove the now-closed refrigeration truck to HQ to be processed. The ambulances and body wagons followed.

A few moments more and all RED agents had cleared out and were headed back to HQ.

As Team Supervisor and operation leader, Zane was one of the last agents to leave the scene. He gave one final appraisal then headed off to the location he'd left his RED-issued Trailblazer.

12

"Double caramel double-blended venti frappuccino up for Willow!" a barista called out.

Yum. Willow went to the Starbucks pickup counter and grabbed her drink, the plastic cup instantly chilling her hand. She hitched higher on her shoulder her purse that was heavy as usual with her small laptop weighting it. Just as soon as she finished drinking her frap she'd head to the library and work on her dissertation defense.

A pair of women vacated a small round table in the corner of the crowded coffee shop and Willow plopped into one of the chairs the moment it was empty. *She scores*, she thought and almost laughed then rolled up the sleeves of her white button-up blouse. She unwrapped and plunged her straw into her frappuccino.

Before she had a chance to take one sip, a man said, "Anyone sitting here?"

Automatically Willow shook her head as she looked up. The place was crowded, and she was lucky to have grabbed a chair, so she didn't mind sharing.

The man smiled when she met his gaze. She started to smile

in return, but a prickly sensation sent goose bumps rising on her arms. Something didn't feel quite right about the way he looked at her with his dark eyes as he took the opposite seat.

He had beautifully carved features and night-black hair. He extended his hand. "Filippo," he said. His accent was clearly Italian like his name.

Willow didn't want to take his hand, but she forced a smile and let him take hers. His was hot and dry and more prickles rolled up her arm. He didn't take his gaze off her and she had to tug to get her hand away from his.

"What is your name?" he asked in his smooth accented voice.

Then she noticed the man didn't even have a cup of coffee.

Zane's and Aunt Becky's words echoed in her head at the same time, telling her not to be too friendly with strangers. She'd always followed her heart and her gut, and both were telling her to get the hell out of here.

"Oops!" Willow faked another smile as she wrapped her fingers around her frappuccino cup and pushed back her chair. "I forgot I'm supposed to meet up with my trainer. He's a former football player and he's so tough. He'll probably make me do extra reps."

She was to her feet and pushing her way through the crowded coffee shop before he had a chance to say a word.

Just as she opened the glass door to let herself out, she caught a reflection—the man was following her.

Willow's heart lunged into her throat. She tossed the frap that she hadn't even sipped into the black waste can beside the exit and swung around the door as fast as she could without running.

You're imagining things, Willow. There's not some man following you. But she looked over her shoulder she saw he was close behind and his long strides were taking him closer to her.

Oh, my God. He was following her. Willow glanced around

and saw a large group of tourists on the Freedom Trail and ran straight into the middle of the crowd.

Immediately she realized she had a new problem. At five-eleven she towered over the group that was mostly comprised of foreign visitors who were at least five inches shorter than her.

The Italian joined the crowd and before she could move ahead, the man cupped her elbow with his hot, dry hand. "Where are you going in such a hurry, Willow?" he said in his smooth voice. He wrapped his fingers around her arm and jerked her to a stop so that the crowd parted around them, leaving them behind.

The sound of her name—that she hadn't told him—coming from the Italian sent cold shooting through her.

Bravado. Confidence. Don't let him know you're scared as hell.

Yeah, right.

She jerked her arm as she whirled and glared up at him. "Let go of my arm or you *will* regret it."

He smiled and tightened his grip as he moved behind her. "You're going to come with me."

She hadn't played basketball for eleven years without knowing how to intentionally foul someone.

With all her strength, Willow rammed her free elbow into the man's gut. At the same time, she hooked her ankle around his and jerked him off balance.

A shout of obvious surprise came from him as her other elbow slipped from his grasp. She whirled on one foot like she was holding a basketball and looking for a good pass. Instead, she let her heavy purse drop from her shoulder, slide down her arm, and into her grasp.

She gripped the straps of her purse in both hands and swung right at the man's face.

Score.

"Fuck!" the man shouted as she nailed him in the face, the

side of her laptop slamming into him with the power of her swing. Blood immediately started flowing from his nose and it was bent at an odd angle now.

At the same time, he'd dropped to the sidewalk, something metal with a dull shine flew from his hand and skittered across the concrete.

She ran.

It hammered at her mind that the man had been holding a gun and that's what had spun away from him. He could have shot her. Why would some strange man want to shoot her?

Willow's heart pounded like mad and adrenaline spiked in her veins, giving her more speed. She rounded a corner, her breath coming in harsh gasp from the fear racing through her. The squeal of tires came from around the corner.

She ducked into a clothing store filled with high racks of dresses and low circular racks of blouses and slacks. The salesperson was busy and at that moment all Willow could think about was hiding. The man had a freaking gun, and she wasn't about to remain in the open.

Willow dropped to her knees and crawled under a rack of shirts and was relieved to see it wasn't a rack with an open center. It had a flat surface above her meant to hold a mannequin.

When she was under the clothing she scrunched up with her jean-clad knees drawn up to her chest and her purse tight against her. She bit her lip to keep herself from breathing too loud.

"Can I help you?" a woman said from somewhere across the store. The salesperson.

Then came that smooth Italian voice, only now it sounded not so smooth, like he was having a hard time talking—probably because she'd broken his nose. Every word he spoke held a bite of fury. "Did a woman come in here? Very tall. Blonde."

The woman hesitated. "How long ago?"

"Now." It sounded like the Italian was also having a hard time not sounding like he was pissed. "Within the last two minutes."

"Definitely not." Willow almost let out a gasp of relief that the woman hadn't spotted her—or at least was covering for her.

The man said nothing in response, and she heard his footsteps heading toward the door. He started speaking in a one-sided conversation and she realized he was talking to someone on a cell phone.

"She got away," the man was saying as his voice grew more distant. "No, I don't know where the hell she went. She wouldn't have escaped if I did." Then the faint words came, "cop" ... "girlfriend."

And then nothing.

Willow slumped against the metal support at the center of the rack. He was gone.

Then she almost screamed when someone parted the clothing in front of her. Relief flooded through Willow again when she saw the salesperson.

"Are you all right?" the woman asked as she extended her hand. "I'm sure that man is gone. Should I call the police?"

"Thank you for not telling him I came in." Willow let the woman help her up. Her head felt a little woozy as she stood. All that adrenaline and being scrunched like she'd been before getting up made for one dizzy blond.

"Police?" Willow shook her head, more to clear it than to say no. "I'm dating a cop. I'll call him," she said when she began to think straight again. She needed to talk to Zane. Somehow, she knew only he could help her. "Can I use your phone? I don't carry one."

The woman reminded Willow of Aunt Becky with her motherly air as she ushered Willow to the back of the store. "You should have a phone for emergencies." The woman glanced over her shoulder. "I don't know what this was all about, but that man looked dangerous. Not to mention all that blood on his face and his shirt."

"You bet I'm going to get a phone now just as soon as I find a store that sells them." Willow swung her purse onto her shoulder as she tried to think of the closest phone store. Her thoughts were pinging all over the place. "I could have been calling for help while I was hiding. Or when I first noticed that man following me."

"Why was he following you?" The woman went behind the sales desk and handed Willow a corded phone. "Did you hit him or something? Blood was practically pouring from his nose."

"Honestly, I don't know who he was." Willow's hands shook as she punched in the number for Zane's cell phone. "He just grabbed my arm and I let him have it with my purse." She glanced at the purse and shook even more when she saw the blood on the corner of it.

"Good job," the salesperson said. "You must have nailed him good." Then the woman moved away, obviously to give Willow some privacy as she made her call.

Willow almost cried with relief when Zane answered, "Steele."

"It's Willow," she said, doing everything she could to keep her voice from cracking. "Something just happened. I'm scared. I have to talk to you. I need to see you."

His voice sounded tight, concerned. "Where are you?"

"I'm—" She tried to focus as the adrenaline rush started to leave her. "Near King's Chapel." It hit her that the man had tried to kidnap her right in front of the centuries-old cemetery next to the chapel.

"Are you someplace safe?"

Willow looked at the salesperson. "What's the address?" she asked the woman, then repeated the address to Zane.

"I'll be right there." He sounded as if he was forcing himself to remain calm. "Don't move."

Willow swallowed. "Okay," she said right before he ended the connection.

"Thank you." She looked at the salesperson as she set the phone on the receiver. "My boyfriend, the cop—he's coming to get me."

The lady nodded. "You'll be safe here."

Willow stayed in the back of the store. The moment Zane walked through the door, she ran to him, threw her arms around his waist, and started shaking.

"WHAT HAPPENED, HONEY?" Zane's throat was tight as he put his arm around Willow's shoulders and guided her outside the store and into the sunny morning.

Zane had parked his work SUV illegally in front of the chapel's burial grounds but had his placard in the window indicating that his vehicle was there for law enforcement purposes.

"Some man." Willow's shoulders were trembling and that scared the shit out of him. It had to be something bad. "He—I think he tried to kidnap me."

"What the hell?" Zane's mind churned as he stopped in front of the gate to the King's Chapel Cemetery. He took Willow by the shoulders, and she met his gaze. She didn't look like she'd been crying but the fear was still in her eyes. "Tell me exactly what happened."

A shot pierced the quiet morning.

Willow gave a cry of pain and surprise, and he barely caught her as she collapsed and blood began to spread, brilliant red against her white shirt.

13

———

Zane's system went on instant overdrive. Heat burned through him, and adrenaline pumped through his body.

He grabbed Willow by the waist and flung them both through the cemetery gates to the ground, causing her to cry out again even as he tried to keep her on her back. He didn't know how badly Willow was hurt, but he had to get her out of the line of fire.

Zane had his Glock out in a second. With one hand holding his weapon, he kept a tight hold on Willow and scooted behind several ancient headstones.

At the same time, he drew his handgun, Zane pressed a switch on his holster for emergency extraction.

The moment Zane pressed that button, a RED extraction unit was notified, and they had already honed in on Zane's location via a satellite link even more accurate than GPS.

Bullets pinged on the metal fence from the direction of the shots. People screamed. An ancient headstone exploded nearby as another bullet missed them.

Zane's whole body vibrated, and he prayed Willow hadn't been seriously shot.

His gut clenched. All that blood on the left side of her chest made it look like she'd been hit damned close to her heart. He glanced at her and saw blood coating her fingers and staining the shoulder of her blouse as she pressed her hand to a wound.

On her shoulder, not her chest.

She sounded like she was talking through gritted teeth as she lay flat on her back on the ground. "Don't worry about me. Just get him."

More shots rang out.

More people screamed in the street.

Fuck.

Zane stayed low as he held his Glock and looked through a pair of headstones. Anger burned through him as he spotted the shooter, a man with a bloody nose, peering around the side of the chapel.

The man swung around and used his handgun to shoot toward the stones where Zane and Willow were hiding. Another ancient headstone exploded, and hard chunks rained down on Willow and Zane.

From his prone position, Zane held his Glock in a two-handed grip and sighted the shooter. The fury boiling inside him had him wanting to kill the sonofabitch. But he didn't know why the hell they were being shot at and he wanted to take the man in for questioning. RED would be here any second.

With two rapid shots, Zane put a bullet through the man's right shoulder, then his left. The screams that followed gave Zane only a little satisfaction as the shooter started to drop and his handgun slid into the street, at least ten feet away from him.

For good measure, Zane shot the man in both thighs. More screams before the man fell on his bloody face.

Hopefully, there was only one shooter since the bullets had

come from one direction and the shots had stopped the moment the man was down.

Zane jerked his RED cell phone out of its holster and pushed a speed dial number. He could already hear tires screeching to a halt on the other side of the fence. "One shooter down," Zane relayed. "He could have another weapon on him. Take him alive for questioning. Not sure if there's a second or third gunman."

He jerked his gaze to Willow and his heart nearly stopped beating. "I've got a civilian down, too," he added before he clicked off and shoved the phone into its clip.

Willow's eyes were closed, and her bloody hand had fallen away from her shoulder wound that was bleeding so badly most of the top half of her blouse was soaked with blood. How close was the wound to her heart?

With the sound of RED agents swarming the area of the park they were in, Zane set his Glock close to his right hand.

"Willow!" He shouted as he patted her face with one hand and pressed his other palm over hers, against the wound.

Fear spiked through him. All that blood—shit. He couldn't let her fall asleep. "Wake up, Willow. Stay with me."

Her eyelids fluttered and of all things she gave a slight smile. "Guess I'll be calling in sick to work."

ZANE'S TEMPLES ached and the sick sensation in his gut grew even worse as he paced the waiting room. Willow had been taken to RED's infirmary because he hadn't been sure whether or not the shooting was RED-related, and the organization had to take special precautions.

What was taking so long? How badly was Willow hurt? There had been so goddamned much blood. He admired her spunk, the way she'd challenged him, and her fresh honesty and easy confidence. He loved how she constantly surprised him like she had with her basketball skills and every dare she made.

Everything about Willow was special and his chest hurt even more as if he'd been the one shot.

Why would anyone go after Willow?

To get to me.

"Zane!"

He snapped his head up and saw Georgina Rizzo and Lexi practically running into the waiting room.

"How is she?" Lexi asked, her green eyes bright with concern. "Is Willow going to be okay?"

Zane dragged his hand down his haggard face. "They haven't told me a goddamned thing."

"It's only been an hour since you arrived, so this isn't a bad sign. Just hold on." Rizzo was still decked out as a mafia girl-friend and holding high heels in one of her hands but wearing snug jeans. "I heard about it the moment you called for extrac-tion—I was in the department." She swallowed. "I couldn't go because of what I'd overheard from Albano, so I knew a Petrelli would be there."

Fire raced through Zane's entire body. "This was a mafia hit?"

Rizzo nodded. "All I overheard was that they were after whoever was responsible for the bust. I found an excuse to leave and went straight to HQ. Then everything went to hell."

"It was Henry." Lexi said and Zane rounded on her and even his ears started to burn. "The information recovery specialists used RED's truth serum on Filippo Petrelli as soon as they brought him in."

"I was there when Lexi got the report," Rizzo said. "Thanks to the serum, Petrelli spilled everything about how they found out Henry was a snitch. The Petrellis tortured Henry the day following the takedown and broke all of his fingers until he told them who'd been responsible for the bust. Then they blew him away."

"They wanted blood—several of the Petrellis went down that night." Lexi touched Zane's arm. "The Petrellis have been following you and Willow the past two days since Henry gave you up." She glanced at Rizzo before looking at Zane again. "They were waiting for a chance to grab her to hurt you."

"Fuck!" Zane almost slammed his fist into a wall in the waiting room. This was exactly why he didn't get into relationships. Someone he cared about could get hurt because of him.

And Willow had been the one to pay for his stupidity. "I shouldn't have gotten involved with her." Zane went to a different wall and pulled his arm back, ready to put a hole through it anyway.

"Don't." Lexi caught him by the elbow, and he cut his gaze to her and he almost growled. "You didn't do anything wrong," she said.

"Like hell." Zane was about to say more but the door to the infirmary slid open and Dr. Kelly walked through.

"She's perfectly fine." Dr. Kelly went straight to Zane and his knees almost collapsed.

"How bad is it?" Zane said in a gravely voice filled with so much he wanted to say and so much anger that he couldn't express right now.

"Considering she was shot in the shoulder and the bullet chipped bone and tore ligaments, it will take her shoulder some time to heal." Dr. Kelly continued, "She's going to be wearing an arm brace and then a sling for a while."

"Goddamnit." Zane couldn't think of enough swear words to express himself right now. "When can I see her?"

"We're moving her to a private room now." Dr. Kelly started to turn to the infirmary doors. "About thirty minutes."

It was the longest ninety minutes of Zane's life. From the time they reached the infirmary to now as he followed Dr. Kelly to Willow's room.

When they reached the door, he almost didn't want to walk in. He sucked in his breath as Lexi said, "Go," and Rizzo added, "We'll wait right here for you."

Zane swallowed and entered Willow's private infirmary room and he wanted to drop to his knees and beg for forgiveness when he saw her pale face, the dark circles beneath her closed eyes, the IV, and the huge brace on her arm.

Even though his feet didn't want to move, he made himself go to her and sat beside the bed. He took her hand and squeezed it. "Honey? Are you okay?"

Hell no she wasn't okay.

Willow opened her eyes and turned her head to face him. She smiled but it was weak, like she was too tired. "They gave me Demerol," she said. "I don't know how long I'm going to stay awake."

"I'm so sorry." Zane pressed his forehead against her hand. "I should never have—"

"Shut up." Willow sounded angry and he looked up and met her beautiful eyes. Anger sparked there, too. "I knew exactly what I could be getting into. Don't you dare insult me by saying you never should have dated me."

Tingles prickled Zane's skin as a strange feeling rolled over his skin. "Willow—"

"I said shut up." She looked angry enough to come out of the bed. "You are not going to dump me because of this. Maybe for some other reason, but not because of your feelings of guilt that I got in the way."

Words wouldn't come to his mind or his mouth. If he said

anything, she'd probably come out of that bed and after him in a flash.

"I'm a big girl, Zane." Color had returned to Willow's face. "I may not always do the right things or make the right choices, but with you I have. If you're going to leave me then it better be a damned good reason because this sure as hell isn't."

"Willow—"

"Do I have to knock some sense into that thick head of yours?" She started to rise out of the bed. "Because I will, Zane Steele. How do you think that creep got his broken nose? I'm not above bodily injury."

To his surprise, he almost smiled as he got up and pushed on her good shoulder to get her to lie back down.

"I can't help but love you." The words came to Zane so easily it surprised him. "Everything about you. But it scares me. This scares me."

Willow's features relaxed and she smiled. "I know."

"You've said that since the first time we met." Zane found himself starting to smile. "Do you know everything?"

"Of course," she said. "And I'm never going to let you forget it."

He bent over her and stroked her hair from her cool forehead. "Never?"

"Nope." She shook her head on the pillow. "I intend to kick your brothers' asses at basketball for a long time to come."

Zane was almost grinning now. "Are you asking me to marry you?"

Her smile was so brilliant it made his heart thump like crazy. "Is that a yes I see on your expression?"

He moved his knuckles across her cheek. "One thing."

She raised her brows. "Watch it ..."

Zane had never smiled so much in his life as he did around Willow. "You haven't told me that you love me."

"Oh, that." She reached up her good arm and caught him by his shirt, bringing him down for a hard kiss.

God, she tasted sweet and womanly, warm and incredible. She only allowed him to draw away slightly. "I love you, Zane Steele. Now say you'll marry me. I promise to get a ring and do it right when I get out of this place."

Zane laughed at the image of Willow on one knee presenting a ring to him. She'd do it, too.

"Yes." He kissed her again. "When?"

"Before I defend my dissertation." She smiled against his lips. "Then instead of Dr. Randolph, I'll be Dr. Steele."

Willow captured his gaze and held it. "Dr. Steele has a nice sound to it," he said.

"Yup."

"I think I've found a way."

She raised an eyebrow. "A way for what?"

"To keep you from picking up strange men in the Common."

Willow smiled and drew him down to her again. "I think you have."

EXCERPT: HIDDEN PREY

1

———

The nightmare had been so damned *real.* Landon Walker sat on the edge of his bed, his eyes bleary and his head aching like a mother. He had to stop trying to find peace at the bottom of a bottle of Jack D, because it only made him feel like hell the next morning. Didn't matter what he did, because he didn't think he'd ever have peace again.

His dream had replayed every last detail of that night when a hit-and-run drunk driver had sideswiped Landon's motorcycle, sending Stacy flying and pinning him beneath the wreckage. A helmet and protective gear hadn't been enough to save her. After he'd managed to get out from beneath the motorcycle, he'd crawled to her, dragging his shattered leg. He could still feel her broken body in his arms.

He ran his hand down his face, the stubble and scar along one cheekbone rough against his callused palm. Fourteen months to the day Stacy had died in the accident, an accident that had been his fault.

Would he ever stop marking time by the date of his fiancée's death?

He turned his head to look at the alarm clock and winced

from the pain the sudden movement caused. Damn. He'd be late if he didn't get his ass out of bed. He didn't work some punch-the-clock forty-hour workweek. But Mondays still sucked.

Early Monday mornings he used to play basketball with a bunch of guys who were in law enforcement. On Friday nights, those who weren't working usually played poker. But after the accident, Landon had pulled away from everything but his job. He still worked out—sometimes excessively—in the fitness room in his home. Not only to stay fit but because the strenuous activity burned off excess anger at himself and sometimes at the world.

With his head still aching, he stepped under ice-cold water in the shower in an attempt to wake up. He braced his hand against the smooth white tiles, his head lowered, goosebumps prickling his skin when he let the water flow over him. He kept the water cold as he washed his hair and soaped his body. When he'd finished, he shut off the water and shook his head, droplets flying before he toweled himself off.

The cold shower had done its job and he felt marginally better by the time he pushed open the shower stall's glass door. He might just make it through today after all. Last month had been the first month he hadn't taken flowers to Stacy's grave. For the first year, he'd visited once a month on the date of her death, but after a year, he'd made the decision to move on to save his sanity. Damned if he knew how.

After he'd dressed in jeans and a faded blue T-shirt, he jammed his Colt .45 into its holster on his belt. He slipped on a white overshirt to cover his weapon then stood in his kitchen and wolfed down a breakfast of toast and scrambled eggs. He stuck the dirty dishes in the dishwasher and headed out.

A light morning breeze slid over his skin when he climbed into his charcoal-gray Ford Explorer. He stuffed his key into the ignition and started the vehicle. He headed down the dirt road leaving his ranch and continued onto the paved road that would take him to Douglas.

He had just enough time to make it to the office and take care of a few things prior to heading to Bisbee to meet with his man who'd been working deep undercover. He'd make the twenty-five-mile drive from his ranch in Sulfur Springs Valley to Douglas and to DHS's ICE office in twenty minutes.

Landon had served as a special agent with the Department of Homeland Security's Immigration and Customs Enforcement Agency for eleven years now and had given himself completely to his career since Stacy's death. He'd always been married to the job and he regretted not being there for Stacy more. Now he lived and breathed his work. What the hell else did he have? The job would take his soul one day and he didn't plan to fight it.

At the office, he spent some time going over aspects of the case he'd been working for months. The Jimenez Cartel's tentacles reached far from Mexico, into Arizona. When they chopped off one arm, another grew to replace it. The cartel had to be cut off at its head. No other way would stop or even slow the activities of the organization that dealt in drugs, death, destruction.

They had to get to Diego Montego Jimenez, known as *El Demonio* to everyone around him. The Demon. The nickname for the bastard fit him like a glove.

Landon headed out of the office in the early afternoon. On his way out, he saw Dylan Curtis, another DHS special agent and one of Landon's good friends. At six-three, Dylan stood a good two inches taller than Landon. He wore a Stetson over his dark hair and his ice-blue eyes were appraising as always.

Dylan paused in front of the entrance. Landon stopped too. "When are you going to join the boys for basketball again?" Dylan mimed going up for a shot. "Had some good games this morning. You need to show up and get your ass back in it."

Landon shrugged. He probably should—one more step toward returning to his life as it had been *before*.

"This leg isn't what it used to be." Landon rubbed his leg that had been shattered in the accident.

"Who gives a shit?" Dylan questioned. "Monday mornings, same time, same place as it's always been. Bring the bum leg."

Landon nodded. "I just might be there next Monday."

"You'd better or I'm gonna kick your ass." Dylan hooked his thumbs in his belt loops. "And don't forget poker this Friday night. It's time you rejoined the living and you might as well go all in."

Landon shook his head. "Maybe."

"Maybe, my ass." Dylan switched subjects as he asked, "On your way to meet Miguel?"

"Yep." Landon nodded. "Any news on the delivery?"

"I'm hoping Miguel can give you a concrete time." Dylan frowned. "All I have is what you do—it's tomorrow, but no time or location."

"I'm sure Miguel has it for us." Landon reached for the door handle. "I'll call you as soon as I get intel from him."

Dylan gave a nod. "Tell the bastard hello for me."

"Will do." Landon pushed open the door and walked into the sunny afternoon toward his SUV before heading to Bisbee, a once-booming town nestled in the Mule Mountains.

His thoughts drifted like the occasional puffs of cottony clouds scattered across the brilliant blue summer sky. The grass along Highway 80 waved in the stiff breeze as he drove by. An unusual amount of rain had made everything greener than usual.

Once he reached the east-side town limits, he guided his vehicle around what the locals had called the traffic circle for decades. The roundabout let him out onto the road that took him on to Old Bisbee after he passed the Lavender Pit and the

Copper Queen Mine. He headed to St. Patrick's Catholic Church to meet with Miguel.

A replica of a church in Ireland, St. Pat's had perched two hundred feet above the floor of Tombstone Canyon for nearly a century. Stained glass windows and marble filled the towering terracotta building. Beneath the soaring ceilings, Jesus Christ on the cross peered down on the congregation, as did the statues of the Virgin Mary and St. Patrick behind the altar.

The icons seemed to look down on him, judging him for his absence from the Church and for his abandonment of God. Hell, God had abandoned both him and Stacy when He'd let her die.

The cool, dim interior of the church smelled of incense and candlewax. The heavy double doors closed behind him as he passed the shallow well of holy water. He did not dip his fingers in the water or make the sign of the cross. He slid into the second to last pew in the back on the far right, so he could see the doors by turning his head slightly.

A tiny woman in black, wearing a white lace mantilla, kneeled in one pew, and an older man leaned against the back of the bench seat in another. The old man's head tilted up so he could stare at the effigy of Christ. The man had a broken look about him, as if this church served as the only solace he would find in this world.

Landon mentally shook his head. Raised Catholic, he had pushed away from the Church once he'd gotten to see what a cruel world it could be. How could a good and just God allow evil men to kill or abuse women and children? Or to force them to serve as sex slaves? How had He allowed someone as sweet and good as Stacy to die as she had? Landon would have given his own life for hers.

Clenching his teeth, he took in the padded wood kneeler at his feet. The kneeler, currently in its upright position, would be lowered by parishioners to kneel on during service or while praying when they came into the church to worship.

For one wild moment he thought about getting down on his own knees and praying to a God he didn't think he believed in any longer. He blew out a breath and ran his finger along a hymnal in the wooden rack in front of him. No, his days of praying were long gone.

He pulled himself out of his thoughts and concentrated on the moment. He checked the time on his cell phone and saw he had arrived a few minutes early. He hoped Miguel wouldn't be late. A devout Catholic, Miguel liked to meet at St. Pat's where he felt closer to God.

Sometimes, as Landon left, Miguel would head to the confessionals at the front right. Landon had worked undercover many times and had been forced to commit sins he wished could be absolved by confessing to a priest.

Landon let his gaze drift over the almost empty pews, noting everything. From the moment he'd arrived, he'd been keenly aware of his surroundings and the double doors behind him. He didn't like having his back to the doors, even though he could casually glance in that direction with his side vision. But if he wasn't safe inside St. Pat's, he didn't know where he would be.

The old man got up from his seat and went to the front of the church, to the left of the altar, and lit one candle among rows of little red jarred candles. Some were lit but most were dark. Landon stared at the flickering candlelight for a moment, remembering himself as just a little boy. In the church he'd grown up in, he'd lit a candle and prayed to God with all he had to save his grandfather who'd been dying from cancer. The first disappointment of many to come, by a God who never seemed to answer his prayers.

The old man stood in front of the candles for a long moment before turning and walking beneath an archway between the walls and thick marble columns. Out of the corner of his eye, Landon watched the man leave, a large swathe of sunlight spilling into the church as he pushed one of the doors open. Then the heavy door eased back into place, leaving it dim again.

Landon checked his cell phone. Late. Miguel, normally punctual to the minute, had yet to arrive. Landon didn't let his mind wander beyond his objective. If he did, he'd spend time dwelling on things that couldn't be changed.

Time passed and Landon's gut tightened. Even though Miguel hadn't made it yet, Landon knew he shouldn't be concerned. After all, he'd forged his way deep into the Jimenez Cartel. When *El Demonio* said, "Jump", Miguel didn't ask how high. He did what he had to do to remain embedded in the organization.

Landon's phone vibrated a couple of times and he read the two short text messages then returned his phone to its holster on his belt. His mother, asking if he would be able to make it for Sunday dinner. One of his sisters, telling him not to let their mother down and to show up on Sundays more often.

He blew out his breath. His family had been pushing him for the past year to make it to get-togethers. He'd drawn away once Stacy had died. Maybe he'd grieved long enough. Knowing he should let go of the past and move on didn't mean it would be easy.

Basketball and Sunday dinners would be a start.

Two more parishioners came in and out of the sanctum. The woman in the mantilla hadn't moved since Landon had entered the church. She kept her head bowed in prayer and her white lace mantilla shadowed her face.

More time passed and the two parishioners who had come in thirty minutes prior lit candles before leaving. Landon checked his cell phone yet again and saw he'd been waiting for nearly an hour. The woman in the mantilla and Landon were now the only people left in the church.

Frowning, he got up from his pew and made his way outside, blinking when he walked into the late-afternoon sunlight. He stood at the top of the steps that went down on either side of him.

The fact that Miguel hadn't shown up wasn't anything to be too concerned about. Any number of things could have come up. Miguel wouldn't call or text anyone at DHS, to ensure nothing could be found to tie him to law enforcement.

A hand with a vise-like grip clamped around Landon's left wrist.

He went for his Colt instinctively as he pivoted before stopping abruptly.

It was the tiny veiled woman who had been in the church since he'd arrived.

He released his grip on the butt of his handgun and left it in its holster. How the hell had she snuck up on him?

The stooped, elderly Hispanic woman pushed the mantilla away from her cheeks and his gaze met small dark eyes nearly lost in a sea of wrinkles. She looked well over a hundred years old, older than his grandmother. Her face reminded him of a withered apple, but her eyes were bright and knowing.

"You will die if you tell her the truth. If you don't tell her, *she* will die." The woman spoke in a low, tremulous voice, in broken English, with a heavy Hispanic accent.

Despite the fact that he didn't believe in crap like premonitions, chills rolled over Landon's skin and he broke out in goosebumps for the second time that morning. He tried to jerk his arm away from the woman's grip but she wouldn't let him go and he didn't want to inadvertently hurt her.

"Remember my words." She released his arm and turned away.

While remaining completely aware of his surroundings, he watched her as she held on to the handrail and slowly walked down the steps. Her words echoed in his head no matter how he tried to force them out.

'You will die if you tell her the truth. If you don't tell her, she *will die.'*

He shook his head and a natural-born instinct to help the elderly had him realizing he should be helping the old woman down the stairs. But she'd already reached the last step when he came to his senses.

In a town where most houses were built on mountainsides, Landon wondered how someone so old and frail could navigate her way around the steep inclines that could give San Francisco a run for its money.

A black Mercedes pulled up in front of the church, answering his question. A newer model vehicle, it had dark-tinted windows and looked as if the owner had washed and waxed it this morning. A Hispanic man of about thirty, wearing a bright white button-up shirt and dark slacks, climbed out of the driver's side and held the back passenger-side door open. He assisted the elderly woman as she slid into the vehicle and closed the door behind her.

The Mercedes was out of place in the small town of Bisbee, Arizona—Landon had never seen a vehicle matching it any of the times he'd been in town. He wondered who the woman was and if she owned the over-seventy-thousand-dollar car in a place where some houses could be bought for close to the same price.

He mentally noted the license plate number and jogged down the steps, heading to his Explorer. When he reached the vehicle, he climbed in and grabbed the electronic tablet he used for work, pulled up the app he needed, then put the plate number into the database.

The car was registered to a Juanita Salcido at an address

farther up Tombstone Canyon. He saved the data. Maybe he didn't need to, but the whole experience had been odd enough that he intended to hold on to the information.

He set down the tablet as he thought about Miguel. Likely he'd been held up, the situation being one where the agent didn't have the ability or freedom to call without compromising himself and his cover.

A gut-deep sensation twisted Landon's insides and he gritted his teeth. Like a blow to the solar plexus, a bad feeling struck him hard.

A real bad feeling.

2

Finally, they were just outside Bisbee. Tori tucked strands of chin-length dark hair behind her ear and leaned back in the shuttle van's seat. She looked ahead at the Mule Pass Tunnel that served as the gateway from the west side of town.

Memories slid back of holding her breath from one end of the tunnel to the other. Girls and boys who grew up in Bisbee made it a game any time they headed out of town.

Like other residents, Tori had often referred to it as The Time Tunnel. It was as though they traveled through time, leaving the world of today and visiting an earlier century.

The van entered the dimness of the tunnel and she resisted holding her breath. Seeping water had stained the concrete walls—the project to maintain the integrity of the structure never ended.

When the van reached the other end of the tunnel, she blinked away the bright sunlight and let out her breath. She almost laughed. Without realizing it, she'd been holding her breath after all.

The shuttle continued on and she leaned forward in her seat, her cell phone in her pocket digging into her hip. Her gaze drifted to take in homes perched on the hillsides and the aging narrow road the shuttle traveled.

Waves of memories rolled over her of her years growing up in Bisbee. She hadn't been able to wait to leave when she had graduated from Bisbee High School. She'd wanted to escape the small town and learn what waited out in the great big world. Now, here she was, running back to it.

Her smile faded. She'd never thought one man could make her whole world crash down around her, chasing her away from her dreams and everything she'd worked so hard for. One man.

Tori ground her teeth. She wouldn't allow this to be more than a temporary blip on her radar. She would go back to her life—only it would be *without* Gregory.

Just the thought of him and what he'd done to her before she'd left him made her feel dirty and her skin crawled.

And now she was running home to Mama.

The backs of her eyes stung. Josie Nuñez Cox had been Tori's safe place, her refuge and, even at thirty-three, she needed her mother more than ever.

Tori put her fingers to her temples. She couldn't believe she'd forgotten not only her laptop, but her six-thousand-dollar clarinet too. She'd left them by the front door of the town house she owned and prayed Gregory wouldn't destroy either in a fit of anger at her leaving. More than likely he wouldn't, because he wasn't prone to physical violence. No, he preferred to sling harmful words when he was angry, beating her down verbally and emotionally.

He'd also expect her to come back for the clarinet, especially. Of the five clarinets she owned, she had paid most dearly for the Buffet Crampon professional. She didn't know how she could survive long without music, but she wasn't going back, not yet. At least her mother still had the old Baldwin upright piano Tori had learned to play on from the age of four and one of Tori's old clarinets might still be around.

If her car hadn't been in the shop, she could have loaded everything most important to her. But she hadn't been able to wait for the car. She'd had to get away from Gregory.

Her gaze drifted out of the window and skimmed over the mountainsides as she fought back tears. The stinging ache behind her eyes slowly dissolved when she turned her focus on her surroundings. She could name the homes of old friends and wondered if any of them still lived there or in town.

The shuttle traveled down Tombstone Canyon, past St. Patrick's Church. She'd belonged to the church from childhood until she'd graduated from high school. She had gone through catechism and had received her first Holy Communion and Confirmation at St. Pat's.

Castle Rock loomed before them while the shuttle continued to Main Street in Old Bisbee. Victorian and European-style homes clung to the hillsides.

The shuttle passed Castle Rock then rounded the bend, continuing down the street between rows of old buildings that had been around since around 1910, rebuilt after a fire had ravaged the town. In the early 1900s, the town had been home to over twenty thousand people, the largest city between St. Louis and San Francisco.

Now the town had less than fifty-five hundred people. It had once been reduced to an even lower population.

Bisbee had nearly died in the 1970s when the mines had closed, but hippies had revived it by restoring old buildings and homes, painting them bright colors and turning the old mining town into an artists' community. The history of the place, plus the uniqueness and quaintness of the town, drew tourists from around the world.

The shuttle driver parked in the lot behind the Bisbee

Convention Center, which had once been the old Phelps Dodge Mercantile. The driver had told her he wouldn't take the van up the steep winding street to her parents' home, so she would climb up on her own. She didn't mind—she'd been a runner in high school and kept in shape by jogging regularly. It would give her a chance to collect herself before she made it to her mom and dad's. She just hoped her dad wasn't there. She needed some alone time with her mom.

After she tipped the driver, she pushed her cell phone deeper in her pocket then tucked her purse into her bright pink travel bag. She still couldn't believe she'd run off without her clarinet and laptop. She'd been so upset she hadn't been thinking clearly when the shuttle had arrived to pick her up and she hadn't remembered she'd left the bag and clarinet until they had been miles away.

She bent to pick up the bag she *had* remembered and her crop top and low-rise jeans revealed her tan belly and back even more. Gregory had always hated her revealing any flesh, including the tattoo on her lower back, just above her waistband. He hadn't liked the idea of other men looking at her, nor did he approve of tattoos on women. She'd had *Klarinette* tattooed onto her skin in college. She liked the German spelling of her chosen instrument, which had been 'invented' in Germany around the turn of the eighteenth century.

Screw Gregory. She slung the bag over her shoulder. She'd wear whatever she damn well pleased.

The heavy bag's long strap dug into her shoulder as she looked around in the waning daylight. A few cars passed while she walked to the old post office, crossed Main Street, then headed back around an old bank building.

She turned onto Subway Street, a quiet one-way street, and walked up a steep road that took her near what had once been an old YMCA. She continued to climb the paved road on the hillside, past the old Central School.

Her phone vibrated in her pocket and she stopped to pull it out. A number she didn't recognize flashed across the display.

She brought it to her ear and answered, "Hello?"

"Where are you?" Gregory's demanding voice hit her like a punch to the chest. "Why haven't you been answering my calls?"

"I have nothing to say to you." She straightened and set her bag on the ground. "We are through."

"The hell we are." The way he spoke hammered every word. "Get your ass home."

Tori gripped the phone tightly. "I'll come back for my things when I'm ready, but we are done."

Before he could say another word, she disconnected the call and jammed the phone back into her pocket. Her face flushed with anger and her footsteps fell heavy on the asphalt as she trudged up the hill toward the point where Shearer turned into Clawson Avenue. The phone vibrated again, but she ignored it.

Near the north side of the arts center, Tori took a shortcut. Once she was farther up the hill, she rounded a vehicle. To her right was a black SUV close to an old white Toyota parked in an alleyway. The growing shadows obscured the cars, out of sight of anyone but someone walking by, like her, which wasn't often in this area.

Two men—one with white-blond hair and Slavic features, and a dark-haired guy with a pencil-thin mustache who looked to be of Hispanic descent—faced a third man. The third man had his back to the white Toyota. He had a slender physique compared to the other two, but she couldn't see his face.

Tori started to turn her gaze in the direction she'd been headed when the men's voices drew her attention again. A fourth man, this one wearing a tailored charcoal-gray suit, stepped out of the back of the SUV. The man had finely carved features and an athletic build.

Something glinted in the fading sunlight and Tori froze. Her heart thudded when the man in the suit pointed a gun at the lone man who stood with his back to the Toyota.

"Death is more than you deserve, Mateo." The suited man's Hispanic accent was heavy and cultured. "But your death will send a message."

Horror gripped Tori as the speaker aimed his handgun at Mateo's chest. It had a long barrel, like one of those guns with silencers she'd seen on TV.

Mateo didn't flinch and he raised his chin. "Your family's reign of terror will end, *El Puño.*"

The man in the suit gave Mateo an appraising look and a smile curved the corner of his mouth. "A dead man's desperate attempt to make his life end with meaning. Pathetic." The man gestured to the ground. "On your knees."

When Mateo didn't move, the other two men grabbed him by the arms and forced him to his knees, facing away from the suited man, his hands cuffed behind him.

Tori stared, unable to breathe, much less comprehend the scene.

The suited man moved closer and put the barrel of his gun to the back of Mateo's head.

A spitting sound, and blood and brain matter sprayed over the white car as Mateo dropped. He collapsed on his side and, in her shock, Tori saw his face had been blown off.

Tori screamed. The remaining three men turned and spotted her. The man in the suit raised his gun and pointed it at her.

She dropped her bag and ran.

Terror ripped through her. Adrenaline pumped in her veins, jacking her pulse, and her blood pounded in her ears.

Oh, God, oh, God, oh, God!

The men had the way down blocked off. She had to run higher on the hillside.

"Get her!" the man in the suit shouted. "Kill the bitch!"

A bullet pierced a stop sign as she passed it, the pinging sound saying it tore through metal.

Tori ran faster. Her heart beat harder, out of control, as if it might explode from fear. She couldn't think, she could only react.

Sounds of heavy footfalls grew louder and she doubled her speed. She could outrun these men. She *had* to outrun them.

She glanced over her shoulder and her fear spiked. Maybe two hundred feet away now, the men each held guns, aimed at her.

Another scream tore from her and she increased her speed. Even though she ran every day, the high altitude and the steepness of the streets winded her.

She threw another look over her shoulder. The men closed in on her. One of them stopped and aimed his weapon. She zigged and zagged, hoping that would keep the men from hitting her. She passed a stone wall beneath a house on the hillside and small pieces of rock exploded beside her.

The sting of the rocks striking her face and arms only made her fight harder to keep running. She prayed for someone to help her but then prayed no one would attempt it so they wouldn't be shot.

These men would kill any witnesses, of that she was certain. She had to outlast them by searching for a place to hide. She thought about the old high school. Could she hide there, in the hope that she wouldn't be found?

The metallic taste of blood filled her mouth and she didn't know how much farther she could make it. This time when she looked over her shoulder, she saw she'd gained ground, now farther ahead of the men.

Her heart pounded and her face flushed, sweat coating her body. Her breathing became more labored and her muscles screamed as she ran higher and higher yet.

She rounded another corner, then an SUV. Just as she ran around the vehicle, rough hands grabbed her, jerking her out of the street. She started to scream when a hand clamped over her mouth.

Panic sent more adrenaline surging through her and she tried to struggle and get away from the strong arm wrapped around her. She kicked, her heel connecting with a shin, and heard the man swear.

"I'm trying to help you." The man's voice was low. "Come on."

She stopped fighting and he released her. She whirled to face a big man with a hard look on his scarred features. He grabbed her hand. Instinct told her he was one of the good guys and she ran with him up a short flight of stairs leading to a small house surrounded by tall shrubs. They ducked in a side door and he shut it behind without allowing it to close hard enough to make a sound.

Her chest rose and fell as she tried to catch her breath, her whole body hot, sweat dripping down the small of her back. Her heart might never stop thundering.

Her gaze swiveled to the man.

He gripped a gun in one hand.

She stumbled in the small kitchen, a cry of fear escaping her. She backed away from the man who held the weapon in his right hand as he peered through the slit in the curtains. Her hip hit a kitchen chair and it screeched over the linoleum. She swung her gaze around, trying to find some kind of weapon.

He glanced over his shoulder and must have recognized the terror in her eyes, staring at his gun.

"I'm a federal agent." He pulled his overshirt aside and relief rushed through her when she saw a gold badge on his belt. He turned back to the window. "You can tell me what the hell is going on once I make sure these bastards are long gone."

"Watch your tongue, Landon Michael Walker," came a voice from behind Tori.

Tori gave a startled yelp as she spun to face a woman under five feet tall, who had to be close to a hundred years old. It was easy to see she'd been a little taller before age and gravity had swiped a few inches from her and caused her back and shoulders to stoop.

"Sorry, Grandma Teresa," Landon said and Tori cut her gaze back to him. He was still staring out of the window. And Tori still trembled.

"Who are you?" Grandma Teresa asked, her tone blunt.

The woman had a strong accent. Polish, Tori thought. She'd had a Polish professor during her undergrad years.

"I'm Tori." She swallowed. "Tori Cox."

"You in some kind of trouble?" the elderly woman asked.

"I-I saw something." Tori's entire body continued shaking. "I—" She put her fist in her mouth and bit down, trying to calm herself.

"No sign of the men chasing you." Landon turned away from the window. "I think you're safe."

She blinked and stared at him.

He frowned. "What did you see?"

Tori couldn't think straight, almost couldn't comprehend the man's question.

"What did you see?" he repeated. "Tell me. Now."

She lowered her hand. Her voice shook when she spoke and she had a hard time getting the words out. "I saw them kill a man."

Landon's expression hardened. "Are you certain that's what you saw?"

"I can't believe it." She brought her shaking hand to her neck. "They shot him. Oh, my God. They shot him."

"I need you to focus." Landon holstered his weapon and grasped her firmly by her shoulders. "Tell me what happened."

"I-I—" Her throat worked. "The alleyway was kind of dark. But I saw them. I wasn't too far from the men. I saw them."

He kept his gaze locked with hers. "Where?"

Her whole body shook harder as all that had happened hit her even more violently. "An alleyway." She tried to focus on her words. "North of the arts center, on the way up School Hill."

He released her and pulled a cell phone out of a holster on his belt. He punched in a single number, likely speed dial. She rubbed her arms with her hands, feeling goosebumps beneath her palms. She bit her lower lip, listening while he reported the possible homicide to the Bisbee Police Department.

When he'd finished talking, his green eyes focused on her. "Tell me everything you saw and heard."

"For heaven's sake, let the girl sit and catch her breath." Teresa shuffled toward a table that barely fit in the postage stamp-sized kitchen as she admonished Landon. "You look like you could use a glass of cold water, young lady." Teresa opened the door of the small older-model fridge.

"Yes, thank you." Tori's mind spun, but she still thought about offering to help the woman.

Landon moved in front of Teresa and took the pitcher out of the fridge. Teresa grabbed a glass out of a dish drainer.

Tori sank into a chair at the table, her body still shaking. Her breathing slowed and her skin cooled some, but her face remained hot.

It was the first chance she'd had to really look at Landon. Her bleary eyes made it difficult to focus, but she forced herself. Anything but think of the man whose face had been blown off.

Landon stood over six feet and wore a blue T-shirt beneath a white overshirt with rolled-up sleeves, which now hid the holstered gun. In spite of the overshirt, she could see his muscular form. He must regularly work out or do something to stay in such great shape. His tough, seasoned look went along with his hard, masculine features and a wicked scar along the right side of his face, from his cheekbone to his jaw. Late thirties, she guessed.

He faced her and her already heated cheeks warmed even more. She couldn't believe that in this situation she'd been taking stock of his assets. She grasped the glass of water he handed her. Her hand hadn't stopped shaking and a little of the water splashed on it.

"Thank you." She drank then set the glass on the table with a light thump. She managed to gather her composure enough to ask, "What agency are you with?"

"Department of Homeland Security." Landon eyed her. "Immigration and Customs Enforcement Agency."

She leaned back in her seat and took another drink of water, hoping it would help settle her nerves. No such luck. "I'm fortunate you were outside."

"I happened to be in the right place at the right time." He pulled out a chair for his grandmother to Tori's right.

"And I was in the wrong place at the wrong time." It surprised her that she was able to do more than stutter.

After the elderly woman had sat, Landon remained standing but leaned over and braced his palms on the table, directly across from Tori.

"Sit, Landon." Teresa spoke in her no-nonsense tone, but the man remained focused on Tori.

"The police are going to need to know what you saw, Tori." It was clear in the way he spoke to her that he wanted to keep her calm, but needed information. "When did it happen?"

"Minutes before you rescued me." She swallowed. "I

walked up the hill and took a shortcut. I saw some men talking." She described the two vehicles and the men the best she could with her mind pinging all over the place. "A fourth man got out of the SUV. He pointed a gun at the man standing against the white car." Fear shot through her once again, as if she were still watching the scene unfolding before her. "It happened so fast."

"Did the men say anything?" Landon asked.

"Yes." She struggled to remember what the men had said. Her thoughts jumbled together and she wrinkled her forehead in concentration. "The one with the gun shouted a Hispanic name." She frowned before it came to her. "Mateo. The man he shot was Mateo."

She put the heel of her palm to her forehead. "Mateo said something and called the man with the gun by a strange name... also Hispanic." She struggled to remember, but it lay just out of reach. "Damn. I can't remember what Mateo called him."

As she spoke, Landon straightened, a granite-hard look on his face she couldn't read. "Mateo. You're sure that's the name of the man who was shot?"

She rubbed her palms on her jeans. "Yes."

"Shit." Landon pulled out his cell phone. He appeared both concerned and furious as he punched in a number and turned away.

"Language." Teresa shook her finger at Landon.

Landon didn't seem to have heard or to have seen her shaking her finger at him. He walked through an archway, out of the kitchen, and into another room.

"Where are you from?" Teresa spoke to Tori in a strongly accented voice.

"I'm originally from Bisbee." Tori slumped in her chair, glad for the reprieve from thinking about what she had witnessed. She reached for her water glass with both hands, sliding her fingers through the condensation. "My parents are Josie and Henry Cox."

Teresa looked thoughtful. "You grew up on Temby Avenue?"

"Yes." It did not surprise Tori that Teresa knew. Tori's family had been lifetime Bisbee residents.

The woman tapped her forehead. "I may be nigh on ninety-six, but the mind's still sharp."

Tori cleared her throat in an effort to speak. "Do you know my parents?"

"I knew little Josie Nuñez since childhood. Back before she married that no-good Cox boy." Teresa met Tori's gaze. "Is he drinking like a fish, same as always?"

Yes, the woman was blunt, but Tori didn't mind the truth. "As far as I know he's still a regular at St. Elmo's."

Teresa shook her head. "A real shame." She eyed Tori. "You don't seem to have come out any worse for it."

"My dad didn't hang around the house much." Tori clenched the glass tighter, trying to focus on Teresa's questions. "Mom mostly raised me."

Teresa frowned. "Josie was a good girl. A real good girl."

Landon walked through the archway, into the kitchen. "I'll be right back." He opened the kitchen door and let himself into the evening.

Moments later, he returned. "I need to get to the scene." He looked at Tori as she held her hand to her throat. "Police are there now, so you'll be safe in my vehicle. Likely the men are long gone. The police will question you and so will I."

"You?" Tori lowered her hand. "Why?"

"I'll explain once we leave." He shrugged out of his white overshirt and handed it to Tori. "Cover up that tattoo and your shirt. If anyone is hanging around and watching from any number of vantage points, we don't want them to recognize you."

Tori stood to take the shirt and slip her arms into it. The shirt hung loosely on her, well past her hips to her upper thighs. She buttoned it up and rolled up the sleeves, concentrating on each task. He pulled a ball cap out of his back pocket and adjusted it for her smaller head.

When he'd guessed the size, he gave it to Tori. "Put your hair up under this."

She took it from him. She wondered if her hands would ever stop shaking. Her chin-length hair took a little extra effort to push under the ball cap. "Can you tell me what's going on? It's something more, isn't it?"

"Questions can wait." Landon turned, bent, and kissed Teresa's cheek before giving her a one-armed hug. "I'll do my best to stop by at the end of the week, Grandma."

"Sooner better than later." Teresa studied him with her watery blue eyes. "I won't be around for long, you know."

"Sure you will." Landon gave her a boyish smile that rubbed away some of the rough edges on his features. "I always knew you'd live forever."

Teresa harrumphed. "Get going, boy."

"Love you, Grandma." Landon opened the door and Tori followed him outside into the near darkness.

READ MORE *HIDDEN PREY!*

ALSO BY CHEYENNE MCCRAY

~

(in reading order)

~Romantic Suspense~

"Sworn to Protect Series"

Exposed Target

Shadow Target coming 2024

Lethal Target coming 2025

Moving Target coming 2025

"Deadly Intent" Series

Hidden Prey

No Mercy

Taking Fire

Point Blank

Chosen Prey

"Recovery Enforcement Division" Series

Ruthless

Fractured

Vendetta

Relentless

"Armed and Dangerous" Series

Zack

Luke

Clay

Kade

Alex (a novella)

Eric (a novella)

~Contemporary Cowboys~

"King Creek Cowboys" Series

The McLeods

Country Heat

Country Thunder

Country Storm

Country Rain

Country Monsoon

Country Mist

Country Lightning

Country Frost (coming winter 2024)

"Riding Tall 2" Series

The McBrides Too

Amazed by You

Loved by You

Midnight With You

Wild for You

Sold on You

"Riding Tall" Series

The McBrides

Branded For You

Roping Your Heart

Fencing You In

Tying You Down

Playing With You

Crazy For You

Hot For You

Made For You

Held By You

Belong To You

"Rough and Ready" Series

The Camerons

Silk and Spurs

Lace and Lassos

Champagne and Chaps

Satin and Saddles

Roses and Rodeo (with Creed McBride from **"Riding Tall" Series**)

Roses and Rodeo (with Creed McBride)

Lingerie and Lariats

Lipstick and Leather

Save by purchasing Boxed Sets

Riding Tall 2 Box Set Volume One

Amazed by You

Loved by You

Midnight with You

Riding Tall 2 Box Set Volume Two

Wild for You

Sold on You

Riding Tall the First Boxed Set

Includes

Branded for You

Roping Your Heart

Fencing You In

Riding Tall the Second Boxed Set

Includes

Tying You Down

Playing with You

Crazy for You

Riding Tall the Third Boxed Set

Includes

Hot for You

Made for You

Held by You

Belong to You

Rough and Ready Boxed Set One

Includes

Silk and Spurs

Lace and Lassos

Champagne and Chaps

Rough and Ready Boxed Set Two

Includes

Satin and Saddles

Roses and Rodeo

Lingerie and Lariats

Armed and Dangerous Box Set One

Includes

Zack

Luke

Clay

Armed and Dangerous Box Set Two

Kade

Alex

Eric

~Romantic Suspense~

Deadly Intent Box Set 1

Hidden Prey

No Mercy

Taking Fire

Deadly Intent Box Set 2

Point Blank

Chosen Prey

Recovery Enforcement Division: the Collection

Ruthless

Fractured

Vendetta

~Urban Fantasy~

"Night Tracker" Series
Coming Soon

Demons Not Included

No Werewolves Allowed

Vampires Not Invited

Zombies Sold Separately

Vampires Dead Ahead

No Cursed Allowed (a novella)

~Paranormal Romance~

"Dark Sorcery" Series

The Forbidden

The Seduced

The Wicked

The Enchanted (novella)

The Shadows

The Dark

Cheyenne Writing as Debbie Ries

~Shawna Taylor Cozy Mysteries~

Cooking up Murder

Recipe for Killing

Pinch of Peril

ABOUT CHEYENNE

Cheyenne McCray is an award-winning *New York Times* and *USA Today* best-selling author who grew up on a ranch in southeastern Arizona and has written over one hundred published novels and novellas. Chey also writes cozy mysteries as **Debbie Ries**. She enjoys creating stories of suspense, love, and redemption with characters and worlds her readers can get lost in.

Chey and her husband live in Arizona with their two Ragdoll cats, two corgis, and two poodle mixes. She enjoys going on long walks, traveling around the world, and searching for her next adventure and new ideas. She also quilts, listens to audiobooks, and builds miniature houses.

Find out more about Chey, how to contact her, and her books at **https://cheyennemccray.com.**

~

Sign up for Cheyenne's Newsletter
to keep up with Chey and her latest novels
http://cheyennemccray.com/newsletter